Praise for *Walk a Black Wind*:

"A very good book . . . Collins handles everything with surety."   —*New York Times Book Review*

"In all of Collins' work, the aspect that first catches the reader's attention is the complexity of the plots. . . . He writes tales distinguished by a strong personal flavor and originality. In these, the typical hard-boiled characteristics are enriched, primarily because of Dan Fortune, the compassionate and philosophical private investigator."   —*Crime and Mystery*

MICHAEL COLLINS
Walk a Black Wind

Carroll & Graf Publishers, Inc.
New York

Copyright © 1971 by Michael Collins

All rights reserved

First Carroll & Graf edition 1989

Carroll & Graf Publishers, Inc.
260 Fifth Avenue
New York, NY 10001

ISBN: 0-88184-500-0

Manufactured in the United States of America

To Deirdre, in trust

CHAPTER ONE

Most of us pass through life without ever meeting real danger or fear. We slide from day to day, and nothing very bad happens. We like it that way, I think, even if we do sometimes feel that life is flat. But fear and horror come to some of us, and we meet it in different ways.

There are some who face it naked and early and come to, terms. Nothing ever scares them again, or even worries them. They are the great, the saints, and the monsters. Then there are some who see fear once and are destroyed. If they go on, they are hollow shells. Most neither come to terms nor are destroyed. They simply endure the moment, survive, and never know how they will meet fear the next time.

The man who came to my one-window office that Thursday in late October had met fear or horror or both.

"Two weeks ago I met a girl," he said. "She's dead, Mr. Fortune, murdered. I want her murderer caught."

He was my height, about five-foot-ten, broad and solid in a good blue pin-stripe business suit under a navy topcoat. His olive-colored face was faintly Latin, clean-shaven and deeply lined, but somehow youthful despite the deep wrinkles. I guessed his age at about forty-five. He held a blue homburg where he sat in my one extra chair, and his thick hair was dark brown and coarse. There was no gray in the hair, and his hat was unusual these days. The business card he placed on my old desk explained the hat: John F. Andera, Sales Representative, Marvel Office Equipment, Inc. Salesmen were among the few who still always wore a hat.

"What was the girl to you, Mr. Andera?" I said.

His eyes were a cloudy blue as if he had been stunned. He looked like a man who has been hit by a train and isn't sure yet what damage has been done. Not sure if he was alive or dead, holding himself together inside, breathing carefully.

"A friend," he said. "I liked her. I had . . . hopes."

He spoke with a kind of stiff, prep-school diction that was not natural to him. The sound of some faint accent underneath.

I said, "What was the name originally? My grandfather was Fortunowski when he got off the ship. Sometimes I miss it."

He didn't smile. "Anderoparte. We came from Corsica. My father changed it for business. Will you take the job?"

"I'll have to know more about it," I said. "You only knew this girl for two weeks?"

He glanced around my cubicle office with its view of an air-shaft wall as if he was surprised I'd think twice about any job. With the shabby office, my rough clothes, and my missing arm, I don't look affluent, and we are a world based on cash and prospects. Andera had expected me to be hungry to work, but he said nothing. He took two newspaper clippings from his pocket, gave them to me.

They were both from *The New York Times*. The first was from yesterday's late edition, Wednesday. An inch from page nine:

WOMAN FOUND MURDERED

Fran Martin, of 280 East Eighty-fourth Street, Manhattan, was found stabbed to death in her bed at 8:30 A.M. this morning by her weekly cleaning woman. Police report that the victim died sometime after midnight last night. No motive is yet known for the brutal slaying of the woman who worked as a cocktail waitress at the Emerald Room on East Sixty-sixth Street. Police are investigating.

The second clipping was much longer, dated Thursday, today, and had run on page two of *The Times:*

MURDER VICTIM DAUGHTER OF
UPSTATE MAYOR

The attractive young victim of Tuesday night's slaying at 280 East Eighty-fourth Street has now been identified as Francesca Crawford, daughter of Mayor Martin J. Crawford of Dresden, New York.

On his arrival at the Plaza, the Mayor of the upstate city stated that he knew of no motive for his daughter's murder, and neither he nor his wife could cast any light on the tragedy.

Mayor Crawford revealed that his daughter had left home three months ago, and had not been in contact with her family since. He could offer no explanation for her living in Manhattan under an assumed name. The Mayor and his wife are now in seclusion at the Plaza.

Police identified Miss Crawford through her roommate, Celia Bazer, who had been away visiting friends on Long Island. The roommate is now being interrogated, but police emphasize they have no leads.

Miss Crawford, first identified as "Fran Martin," was found stabbed in her bed—

The rest was a repeat of the first story, with more words but no more facts. I handed the clippings back to John Andera.

"Any ideas why she was killed?" I asked him.

"No, none," he said. "I met Fran two weeks ago today at a party. She was alone, I took her to a late dinner. I liked her. I took her out twice more. We . . . got along. She seemed much older, more mature, than she really was."

"How old was she?"

"Twenty, Mr. Fortune. Just twenty. I went away a few days on business this week, returned on Wednesday for a date with Fran. She didn't show at the restaurant. I was angry, so didn't call her. Today I saw that second story." His thick hands shook. "She had been using a false name. Then she was dead. I had hoped . . . well, that we . . ." He stopped.

"You can prove you were out of town?"

"Yes, of course." He had expected the question, and he anticipated my next one. "I'm not married, I have no jealous women, and I don't know if she had other men. I don't know anything, that's why I want you. I can pay well."

"For a girl you hardly knew?"

"How long does a man have to know a girl to know he likes her? I liked her a lot! I'll pay you a thousand dollars in advance, another thousand when you bring in her murderer!"

His voice was still steady, but inside he was bleeding hard where it didn't show but hurt just as much. Inside, he was crying for a girl who hadn't even given him her right name. Then, that wasn't so unusual in the fast world of New York.

"That's a lot of money," I said. "You could get a big agency for that, and the police will handle it well enough."

"The police have too much work, and I don't want Fran lost in a big agency's computers. I want a man who will work for Francesca. I want to do something!"

"It's still a lot of money," I said.

"Yes, it is. Because I want to make you take the job, and because I want my name kept out of it. I don't want to be involved." He said it bluntly. Either he was naïve or bolder than he looked.

"Even though you can prove you were out of town?"

"I'm not worried about being thought guilty," he said. "It's just that a young girl, a salesman, a few weeks, you understand?"

I understood. The newspapers, and his office people, would have a fun-time with it. We love to see dirt.

"All right," I said. "In murder, I have to work with the police. If I can't keep you out, I'll tell you first."

Andera thought for a moment, then nodded, and stood up. He counted ten hundred-dollar bills from his wallet. They were all new bills, he'd come prepared from his bank.

"I'll come here for any reports," he said.

When he had gone I thought about him. He had paid me more than I was worth on any market, and I had a hunch that he knew it. Had he decided how much it would cost to make me take a case I didn't quite believe? Maybe, but did that mean that his story wasn't true, or only that he was afraid I wouldn't think it was true?

The only way to know was to go to work, and I could always use two thousand dollars. I called Centre Street. They told me Captain Gazzo was on the case. It figured—a mayor's daughter. Gazzo agreed to meet me at The Medical Examiner's Building on the East River.

CHAPTER TWO

I walked across town in the autumn afternoon sun, the sharp October wind blowing through my old duffel coat. A wind that had been blowing hard all week, the whole city walking bent.

Captain Gazzo was at one of the crypts in the basement autopsy room when I walked in. The dead girl in the crypt had not been beautiful, yet there was something very alive about her face even in death. Her long, dark hair framed a face of high, broad cheekbones, and a proud nose like a hawk. There was an Oriental shape to her dark brown eyes. She wore no make-up at all. It made her seem older.

Gazzo said, "I know all the violence, but I never get used to the young ones. Especially not the girls."

"Women's Lib wouldn't like that," I said. "Male prejudice, feeling worse because women are toys, weaker."

"Maybe they're right," the captain said. "Maybe I do feel worse because it's a waste of what some man should have had. A girl should be alive to produce kids for him, or be a decoration to be protected. A girl is our loss, a dead boy is his own loss."

Sometimes I still wonder where it comes from, Gazzo's flow of words that can drown a prisoner. He says he knows—from thirty years of talking to himself.

"Anything besides the knife wound?" I asked.

"That's all. Once through the heart. She never even woke up. The only other mark is this."

He moved the dead girl's long hair. She had a thick,

12

three-inch scar from under her right ear to her jawbone.
An ugly, livid scar like a bullet furrow.

"It's old," Gazzo said. "When she was around three,
the M.E. thinks. The roommate says she wore her hair
tied back, showed the scar. Flaunted it, you know?
Makes you wonder."

The scar made her broad face seem harder, older,
especially with no make-up at all.

"Anything else in the M.E.'s report?" I asked.

"No. A healthy girl, no bad habits, no evidence of
any recent sex, no bruises. An outdoor type, the M.E.
thinks: from her tan, wind-roughened skin."

"Can we talk in your office?" I said.

I wanted to leave. The young ones bother me too.
Usually, it's the very weak or the very strong who die
by violence so young. I wondered which she had been.

The light is always artificial in Captain Gazzo's office,
the shades drawn. He says it fits better with his work.

"How'd you get on this, Dan?" he asked as we sat
down.

"I knew the girl a little," I lied.

I'm a good liar. I've practiced in a lot of places where
liars have to be good, but knowing when a man is lying
is part of Gazzo's trade. That's one reason I always
work with the police. I need them more than they need
me, and by working openly most of the time, I have a
better chance of being believed in my lie when I don't
want to work in the open with them. I had the convic-
tion that John Andera's out-of-town alibi would check
out, and that if the police hounded him all he would
do was close up and pull out.

"Another charity case?" Gazzo said. "What do you
live on?"

"Very little," I said. "What can you tell me, Captain?"

"Not much. She was in her bed, stabbed once with a
long, thin knife. If a killer knew where to push to miss

bone, the knife would go through like a hot finger through butter. A very efficient weapon, and this killer pushed on target."

"Around midnight on Tuesday?"

"Give or take an hour. No one saw or heard anything, even though people were awake in apartments on both sides."

"How'd the killer get in?"

"No sign. Apartment's on the top floor. No fire escape. Nothing on the roof. The girl's door was on the chain, one window was open. It's risky, but he must have climbed down from the roof without a rope. An expert, or a lucky amateur. Nothing in the place that didn't belong to the girl or her roommate. A very neat job."

"What do you have to go on?"

Gazzo shrugged. "Theory, Dan, and that's about all. A two-bit killing like we get every day. She just moved into the place three weeks ago, told the roommate nothing—not even why she was using a phony name. Wasn't there much, but was alone most of the time when she was. We're looking into her actions, but she didn't have time to do much here. So far, she looks like a solitary kid who did nothing."

I said, "She used a false name, but moved in with a girl who knew her? That's kind of odd."

"Maybe," Gazzo said. "Meanwhile, we go on routine. Some drawers were open, and her handbag was gone. No money around, and she had some. No address book."

"Probably it was in the missing handbag," I said. "Just robbery? Some scared junkie? Or a real pro?"

"It's possible. I don't much like the quick killing for that, or the entry for some junkie, but it happens. Or maybe she was just a runaway girl who mixed in wrong company. The parents are due here any time. I'd like to know more about the time between when she left home, and three weeks ago."

"Okay if I hang around?"

"Hang around," Gazzo said.

They came into the office with the confidence of power in a small city. Rulers in their world, and, like most people, they carried their world with them. It was there in the fine suit and imposing presence of Mayor Martin J. Crawford, and in the mink Mrs. Crawford wore over a slim black suit, despite the heat of Gazzo's office, as if she were making a brief, royal visit. There in their dry eyes and emotionless faces—public faces that looked only at Captain Gazzo.

"Can we take her, Captain?" Martin Crawford said.

He was well over six feet tall and two hundred pounds. His soft hands moved when he spoke as if giving orders. He had a lawyer's eyes that took in everything, but held the results of his judgment to himself until he was sure of where the advantage lay for him in any situation.

"You can take her home," Gazzo said.

Crawford nodded, and then stood there. His lawyer's eyes were clear, but his big body didn't seem to know what to do next. Paralyzed by an event that didn't relate to the world he understood.

"Martin?" the wife said. "You'll call the funeral people?"

"Yes," Crawford said, reminded. "Of course, Katje."

The wife watched him as he went to a telephone. She was a tall, dark-blonde woman about forty. Thin and athletic-looking, she played a hard game of tennis or golf I guessed. No prettier than her dead daughter, her handsome face was thinner, and she must have been a patrician dazzler at twenty among cuter, more girlishly pretty girls. Her upright bearing made me think of medieval ladies who defended the castle when their lord was off to the wars.

She said, "We thank you, Captain. We . . . don't

really know what to do. She was our oldest, Francesca. We . . . we'll always wonder why. What happened? Did it have to?"

"We'll find out what happened, Mrs. Crawford," Gazzo said.

She gave a small shrug, as if to say that she knew Gazzo would find the killer, yes, but would that really tell her what had happened? Or really why?

Martin Crawford put down the telephone. "They'll meet us at the . . . morgue, Katje."

The word "morgue" sounded painful, and Crawford sagged in the hot office, his big face all loose flesh. Mrs. Crawford touched his shoulder. I placed her face and manner—her name was Katje, and she was from up-state New York: a patroon. One of the Dutch aristo-crats. Crawford patted her hand.

"We don't know why she left home," the big man said. "We don't know what she was doing. They have their own minds, the children today. We teach them to think, and they think in ways we can't even know, much less understand."

Gazzo said, "You can't tell us anything?"

"Nothing we can think of," Katje Crawford said. "Francesca was always our difficult child. I never seemed to reach her after she was ten."

"Pigheaded!" Martin Crawford said, the anger as much for himself as for the dead girl. "Sometimes she just sat and stared at us. The best one, I suppose. The best child is often the worst for the parents. A child's standards and her parent's standards are often very dif-ferent, and if the child is tough, they battle."

"You battled a lot with her?" I asked.

They both looked at me for the first time. Martin Crawford nodded.

"All the time. On everything. She even opposed me on public issues. Housing, conservation, crime fighting."

"When did you hear from her last?" Gazzo said.

"After she left we didn't hear at all."

I said, "Three months? Did you look for her?"

"No," Crawford said. "She left a note saying she had gone on a trip. No reason, nothing about where or why."

"She had a scar," I said. "Like a bullet wound."

"A childhood accident," Mrs. Crawford said.

Gazzo said, "Mr. Fortune just wonders if it could have any bearing. So do we. Did someone shoot at her?"

"Martin shot by accident. She was two-and-a-half," Mrs. Crawford said, and she looked at me with a question in her blue eyes. "You called this man 'Mister' Fortune. Isn't he one of your policemen, Captain?"

"A private detective," Gazzo said. "Working with us."

"Private?" she said. "I don't understand. You mean someone hired him? Why? Who?"

"I knew Francesca, Mrs. Crawford," I said. "I met her here in New York. I want to help."

"Help?" she said. "Yes, I see. Thank you."

Gazzo said, "Can either of you think of anything in your daughter's life before she vanished that could help us?"

"No," Martin Crawford said. "I mean, where do we start?"

"In twenty years," Mrs. Crawford said, "how do we pick out what could help you? Francesca was unusual in many ways—busy, too silent, good in school, intense on her own projects. But she was normal, too, with a lot of friends. Some we knew, some we didn't. Nothing stands out, Captain. Perhaps if you had specific questions, but until you do . . . ."

Both Gazzo and I knew they were right. If nothing stood out in their minds, until we had some ideas it would be like shooting fish in a very large barrel.

Martin Crawford said, "She's dead, and what can we do? What's the use of power and money if we can't stop chance, can't control life? What do we do?"

"We go on trying to control life," Gazzo said.

Crawford nodded, and they stood up. The wife went out first—to claim her daughter. We hadn't learned much. Maybe there wasn't much to learn. Just another small-time murder?

CHAPTER THREE

Night was falling fast—the way it does in late autumn—over the East Eighty-fourth Street block where Francesca Crawford had lived briefly as Fran Martin. The wind seemed to have dropped, as if the tree-lined street was walled in from the turmoil of the rest of the city. The East Side can be like that, while the West Side throbs and boils.

The dead girl's building was a small brownstone, neater than West Side brownstones. There were flower boxes in the windows instead of milk cartons and shirtless men. I got no answer to my ring, and the vestibule door was locked. Sure that I was alone, I used my thin square of stiff plastic to open the spring lock. On the top floor I used my ring of keys to enter the silent apartment.

A thin, dusty light filtered over shiny, tasteless furniture of the kind that comes with good furnished apartments and tells you nothing about the occupants. The living room was large, there was a full kitchen, a dining room, two bedrooms, and two bathrooms—$400 a month, at least.

One bedroom was cluttered, with two closets full of clothes for a young woman who went many places but had little taste beyond showing off what had to be a sensual figure. Make-up was thick as a forest on a dressing table, the bed was covered by a spread, and a small desk looked barely used. Paycheck stubs showed that this was the bedroom of the roommate, Celia Bazer. She worked for Bel-Mod Fashions, Inc., and was paid too much to be anything less than a model.

The second bedroom was bare and spartan. There was no make-up anywhere, not even in the bathroom, and fewer than ten dresses in the two closets. The closets were oddly segregated. One held three sleek cocktail dresses, some high heels, and an evening wrap. The other had only bright, loose, casual dresses, slacks, sandals, mannish shirts, a pair of red-stained jeans. All airy and informal, with a sense of youth and independence. The bed was covered with another spread, and there was the same small desk—but used.

The desk was littered with guides to New York, theater programs, nightclub napkins, and paycheck stubs from the Emerald Room. The checks were small; Francesca Crawford had made little money. Nothing went back farther than three weeks. The bureau drawers told me no more. No slips, no girdles, no brassieres, and only four pairs of bikini underpants—a modern girl. The only jewelry was some silver and turquoise pieces—earrings, a necklace, two bracelets. Good, handmade Indian jewelry, but new and shiny, and with nothing to show where it had come from.

As if Francesca Crawford had been on another planet since leaving home three months ago. Unless there had been some clue in her missing handbag. Had the bag been taken to hide where she had been, what she had been doing? Or was it simple robbery? Or, maybe, to suggest a simple robbery?

I turned to the bed. A killer can often become careless at the instant of killing, leave some clue. I pulled back the spread, and got a surprise. There was no blood on the bed.

I went back to the roommate's bedroom, stripped off the cover from that bed. The blood was on this mattress —and a deep tear where the long knife had passed through the dead girl. Francesca Crawford had been killed in the wrong bed.

* * *

The super of the building was a small man who looked me up and down, stared at my duffel coat and missing arm. He had a belligerent air, as if he would belch in your face to prove that he took no guff from anyone. I asked him if Francesca Crawford had had many callers.

"You a cop? With that arm?"

"Private," I said. "Her family wants to know how it happened, what she was doing, who her men were."

His narrow face almost sparkled. The kind of animal thrilled by secondhand pleasures, other people's pain. He rubbed at his jaw. "Said her name was Martin here. Not bad-looking except for that scar, but a funny one. Alone most of the time, never talked much. I had ideas about her and the roommate, only the Bazer kid had plenty of men."

"Francesca Crawford didn't have men?"

"I only seen two in three weeks, then just a couple times. No parties, no gang, no steady like most girl kids."

"Who were the two you saw?"

"One guy forty or so, Dago-looking, but real dressed up. Gray hair, small. Never saw him with her, but he went up a couple times, asked once if she was home."

"The other one?"

"Big, blond guy, maybe thirty," he said, and his eyes were excited. "Saw him the night she got killed, around five P.M. He asked for Bazer first, then the Crawford girl. Wanted to know if I knew where they were. I didn't. I told the cops."

"How about a man about forty-three, short but broad?" and I described John Andera in full.

"Never saw one like that."

"Any women?"

"Nah." No fun in peeping on women with women.

"You heard nothing the night she died?"

"I told the cops. Not a thing."

"And you hear everything, don't you?" I said.

He slammed the door in my face, but I felt better as

I went out into the now dark evening, and headed for the subway. I'd let him know what I thought of him. I was imagining him back in his room cursing me when I turned north on Lexington Avenue and saw the man behind me.

It was dark, and there were a lot of people on the sidewalk. I couldn't get a good look at him, but I was sure he was tailing me. I didn't recognize his clothes: dark, almost black, with a cheap-looking topcoat, and a hat pulled low. To be sure, I turned off the avenue and walked toward the Park. He came behind me, dropping back on the side street where there were fewer people. I did a few sharp turns. He was still on my trail when I turned back toward Lexington. I reached the avenue, and ducked into a doorway around the corner.

He didn't appear. I watched the corner, but no one like him came around after me. I waited five minutes, then took the subway downtown.

Maybe I'd been wrong.

The Emerald Room had just opened when I walked in. Behind its anonymous façade it was a beautiful place of small rooms with deep leather booths, stiff white tables, decent light to see your food by, a real fire against the October chill, and a small, quiet bar. The *maître* took one look at my old duffel coat, and came fast.

"Yes, sir?"

"I'd like to talk to the manager."

"About what?" He was half-curt, and half-relieved. I was a nobody, but at least I wasn't asking for a table.

"A former employee."

"I handle the personnel. What former employee?"

"Francesca Crawford," I said. "Or Fran Martin, I guess."

He froze solid. "The police have asked all, and been told all we know."

"Was there any trouble with her? How about men?"

"She was a quiet, efficient girl. We liked her. Now do I have to call the bouncer?"

His eyes flickered to my left where I saw a muscular middleweight in a loose suit watching us both. I left.

I stopped in a diner on Eighth Avenue near my office for my dinner. If you know an area of New York, you can learn the specialty of each diner, and can eat pretty well for little money by picking the right diner on the right day. Here, on Wednesdays, it was kidney stew, and I thought about Francesca Crawford while I ate. Gazzo was right, there wasn't much to go on. Three weeks is a short time, and that's all she'd had in New York as far as I knew. The roommate, Celia Bazer, might know more, but meanwhile I wanted to look a little farther back.

I saw no sign of anyone following me to the branch library. The library is a detective tool most people forget. It would tell me more about Mayor Martin J. Crawford. I got *Who's Who in America*. The entry wasn't long, Dresden was only a small industrial city:

Crawford, Martin James: Mayor, Dresden, N.Y. Born Dresden, N.Y., April 14, 1920. Ed. private schools, Cornell Univ., Cornell Law. M. Katje Van Hoek; four children. New York State Bar, 1945. Lawyer, Dresden City Council, 1948–50. Elec. New York State Assembly, 1950–56. New York State Atty Gen's Office, 1957–62. Estab. law firm Vance, Crawford and Cashin, 1962. Elec. mayor of Dresden, N.Y., 1964. Dresden Plan (strict Welfare control), 1966. Dresden Crime Comm. estab. 1968, under dir. of Carter Vance and Anthony Sasser, with mayor as chmn. Re-elected 1968. Dresden Plan for welfare control opposed in various court actions, abandoned, 1969.

I closed the book, and thought about Mayor Martin Crawford. A local Dresden boy, and the schools indicated from a "good" family, probably some money.

There was influence, and more than a little ability, in a plum job like City Council lawyer at twenty-five. Until 1962 he had gone the statewide political route. After 1962 it had been private practice and local politics— the bigger fish in the smaller pond. From the sound of the Dresden Crime Commission, and the "Dresden Plan" to crack down on welfare rolls, Crawford was an anti-crime crusader and a conservative reformer. Men who crusade and reform make enemies.

I looked up the number of the Eighty-fourth Street apartment, and called from the library. I got no answer. Either the police still had Celia Bazer, or she was off somewhere, and there wasn't much I could do until I talked to her. I had a thousand dollars in my hands, and I thought about my girl, Marty—Martine Adair, who gives me a lot and gets little in return. I hadn't seen her for a week. She was busy with a new show, a featured role at last, but maybe she was free tonight. I called the theater. Marty wasn't free.

So I went to the bar where my friend Joe Harris was on duty, and had a few Irish whiskies. I even paid. I talked with Joe for a couple of slow hours, then went home. In bed I lay awake quite a while. I thought about the murder of the daughter of an anti-crime, conservative mayor. A girl wasn't killed without a reason—or maybe she was. We live in a violent time, and I guessed that, statistically, more people were killed by unknown strangers than were killed for politics.

CHAPTER FOUR

I woke to a gray day and a throb in my missing arm. I don't often think about the arm, but it's on solitary gray mornings when I do. I ask myself how a man goes on without a part of himself. I never get an answer.

So I got a cigarette, lighted my gas radiators, plugged in my ready coffee, and called Marty. She didn't answer. I wasn't surprised, she'd be too busy until her show opened. There was nothing to do but go to work, and over my coffee I tried to work up the necessary enthusiasm, or sense of duty.

I don't like murder, I know it can't go free, but there's still no pleasure in an eye-for-an-eye, in adding more pain. In a world that lives with legal murder——call it defense, or protection, or a crusade for peace and justice, or what you will——it's hard to work up real hate for some desperate, at least half-crazy fool. I can hate many people, but most simple murderers aren't among them. When you hound them into the light, they're too often pitiful creatures who acted more from fear than from hate or greed. I know that doesn't help if you were close to their victim, and it wouldn't help me if my child had been killed, but it's still true.

The brownstone at 280 East Eighty-fourth was bleak in the gray morning, the wind blowing the last leaves from the trees that stood ringed by their little private fences. I had an odd vision——once man had skulked vulnerable among great forests of towering trees, and now the few trees stood vulnerable among forests of indifferent people.

My ring was answered this time, and I went up. A tall, full young woman waited for me. She was dark-haired, pretty, and more female than the dead Francesca Crawford. I guessed her age as twenty-five-plus, and her prettiness was mostly youth, so she didn't have much time. She wore a blue robe.

"Miss Celia Bazer?" I asked.

"Yes. You're more police?"

"Dan Fortune, a private detective."

"But I don't know anything! I told the police!"

"I just want to talk," I said. "Can I come in?"

"In?" she said, stepped back. "Yes, come in then."

Suitcases littered the living room, and a trunk stood open. I could see empty closets inside her bedroom.

"Home to Dresden," she said. "I don't stay here now. One year in the big city for fame and fortune. I didn't make much fortune, and I don't like this kind of fame."

"You and Francesca were old friends in Dresden?"

"Not so old. A couple of years before she went away to college, a few months when she came back. Her father is the Mayor, mine runs a shoe store."

She resumed her packing. The robe did little to hide her body. She didn't seem to care. I sat down.

"Why was Francesca using a false name?" I asked.

"I don't know. She never said. She just called me one day, asked if I had room, and when I had she moved in."

"You don't know where she'd been before here?"

"I know she was in the city, some other place."

"Was she scared? Hiding?"

"Fran didn't scare. Look what it got her. I scare."

She went on working steadily as if she had to meet some specific time schedule.

"Did she have many visitors?"

"Carl Gans twice for dates. Mr. Dunstan came around a few times after her. That's all. It was weird, alone so much."

"Who are Gans and Dunstan? Can you describe them?"

"Carl Gans works at the Emerald Room. Your height, but heavier. A real rough face, and maybe forty-five. Mr. Dunstan is a smaller man, same age, nice. He looks rich, but I don't know what he does. His name's Harmon, lives in Hempstead."

"Was she involved with either of them? Or both?"

She stared at me. "If you mean was she making out with them, I wouldn't know. She never let them bring her home up here. I think she was tough to get into bed. The tiger type, battle all men."

"How about a big, blond man about thirty?"

She closed her last suitcase. "No, I don't know."

"A John Andera?" I described Andera.

"No one like that I saw."

"Why did she keep her dressy clothes so separate?" I said.

She straightened up. "You noticed that? I don't know why. I think someone gave her the dressy stuff. All she brought was those junk clothes. I never could figure Fran out. She could have had anything, the best clothes by the ton, but she never had much even at home. The bare necessities."

"The rich don't need to buy to feel secure."

"Maybe not," she said.

She went into the bedroom, and realized that all her clothes were packed. She came back out, took off her robe, and in her bra and pants began to pick a dress from a suitcase. The new indifference of youth to modesty is a healthy thing, I guess, so I didn't look away. It wasn't easy; I'm not a youth.

"This place costs money," I said. "Where did she get it?"

"She had it in the bank. I guess her bankbook was in that handbag the . . . that was taken." She was dressed, and said, "Can you help with the bags? With that arm?"

"I can take two if they're not bulky."

I took two slim bags in my one hand, and struggled down the stairs behind her. The trunk would be picked up. On the sidewalk we lined up the bags. She looked at me.

"I don't know what happened to Francesca, Mr. Fortune," she said. "She never told me anything. I'm sorry."

I had the sudden feeling that she was waiting for me to walk away before she flagged down a taxi.

I said, "I can reach you in Dresden?"

"Sure, anytime. My folks are in the book."

"Well," I said, smiled, "thanks for talking to me."

She smiled too, and I walked away toward Third Avenue. When I was out of sight, I looked fast for a taxi. It was midmorning, a good hour, and I got one quickly. In luck.

"Park here," I said to the driver. "Soon I'll say follow that taxi. You want to get the jokes over first?"

"It's your money," the driver said.

We were parked where I could see Celia Bazer. She got her taxi soon. It came across Third Avenue, went on to Second, and turned downtown with me behind it.

Celia Bazer led me to the Cooper Hotel on East Eleventh Street. A cheap hotel with no doorman. Instead, a tall, blond man came out to meet the Bazer girl. Tall and husky, he was handsome in a heavy way. About thirty or so, he seemed to pose as Celia Bazer paid the taxi, conscious of his face and build. His clothes were sleek and studied—a soft gray jacket, darker gray slacks, a pale blue shirt open at the neck to show fine blond chest hair, and pale blue suede shoes. They each took two bags into the hotel.

I paid off my cab, and walked toward the hotel. A green Cadillac came slowly along the street behind me, passed me, and double-parked just beyond the hotel. No one got out. A lone man in the Cadillac was interested in his rearview mirror. I stopped and watched him for a time in a store window next to the hotel. He started up, drove off, and I went into the hotel.

Celia Bazer and the blond man weren't in the lobby. I knew the desk clerk: Willy Hassler.

"Hey, Dan, after me?"

"The blond man just came in, Willy. Who is he?"

Willy Hassler and I had run in the same paths of juvenile theft when we were boys in Chelsea. I only lost my arm from it, Willy lost ten years. Now he was a desk clerk in a cheap hotel. It didn't depress him. He'd lived a lot lower.

"Four-oh-nine, Frank Keefer," Willy said. "Registered from Albany, but it could be phony—he thought about it when he wrote. Been here four days. The woman's new to me."

"Can I listen without bugging their room, Willy?"

Willy closed his eyes. "Four-oh-nine? Yeh, there was a door into four-eleven. And it's empty, four-eleven. Go up."

"I'll send you a bottle of the best, Willy."

"If you got a client, make it cash."

"I'll send something," I said.

I felt cheap as I rode up in the shaky elevator. But a thousand dollars, even two, is something a man has to learn to hang on to if he's middle-aged and never hung on to anything. Self-interest is the game, especially by the mid-forties.

Inside room 411, I put my ear to the plywood panel that now covered where the door to 409 had been. They must have been just on the other side. Celia Bazer was talking. There was anger in her voice, and something more—fear? Or love?

"What do you want from me, Frank?"

Frank Keefer's voice was deep and smooth. "Maybe I just want you after all, Cele."

"Sure. Four years of us, then Francesca and her daddy came into your big eyes, and good-bye for me!"

"Leave Fran out, Cele. We busted up, I told you."

"Maybe you busted up just Tuesday night! The hard way. You want to keep me quiet. You and Joel hate trouble, right?"

"Leave Joel out, too," Keefer said, his voice a little ragged this time. "Fran told me to get lost before she ever left Dresden. You remember that. I never saw her again."

Celia Bazer's voice laughed. "Sure, you came down here just to find me. Surprise, Francesca was living with me! Did you come to try for her again, the jackpot? Maybe it looked like you had a chance. Maybe you got afraid of what I could tell her. Maybe you made a big mistake!"

I could almost feel the threat hanging in the silence inside room 409 on the other side of the thin panel. Frank Keefer's deep voice broke it:

"You have a short memory, you know, Cele? Your face was bad the time I busted it. It could look a lo: worse."

Her voice was thin. "You don't scare me. *You're* scared!"

But Celia Bazer was scared. It was there in her voice. Keefer scared her—and excited her. That was in her voice, a thickness of desire. She was afraid of him, and she wanted him, too. He heard what I did in her voice.

"Come here," his voice said.

The sounds on the other side of the panel were meaningless except in my mind. I imagined them, a man and woman close together. I saw Keefer holding her roughly, because that would be his pose. Her head was against his shoulder. The need in her voice was now stronger than the fear.

"You were really through with Fran, Frank? All over?"

"Three months ago, Cele. I had plans, sure. You can't blame a man for trying for the bonanza. But she tossed me over, and what does Frank Keefer do against the Crawfords? I told Joel the hell with it, I wanted you. I mean it."

His voice didn't convince me, not all the way, and I imagined his eyes not quite looking at her as she looked up at his face. But that was a projection of how I would act. Keefer was probably looking straight at her and smiling.

"Frank?" her voice said. "What happened to Francesca?"

"Don't know, baby. I got down here Tuesday. I went to your place, no one was there. I called Bel-Mod, they said you were out of town. Wednesday night I went to see if you were home yet. The cops were there, I heard Fran's name. I got out. Yesterday, I saw the story in the paper."

Beyond the wall he began to pace. "She'd been strange a while up in Dresden. Sort of keyed up. When she broke off, she said I was just another big fake. I was mad, so was Uncle Joel—all his big plans for getting in with the Mayor. He got drunk, had a fight with Fran. It was the last I saw of her."

Keefer stopped pacing, and there was no sound or movement on the other side of the wall. Until Celia Bazer spoke.

"Let's go home, Frank. Get out of this city."

He didn't answer, but I pictured him nodding, and he picked up the telephone. He asked for a bellhop. I left room 411, and went down to the lobby to wait.

They came out of the elevator with an ancient bellman who struggled with three bags. Frank Keefer carried the other two bags—Celia Bazer was his woman again. While he paid, I went out ahead of them, and ran to the corner to try for a taxi. The first three were taken. I looked back and saw Keefer loading the bags into a flashy red Buick convertible. I saw something else, too.

As an empty cab stopped for me, a man in a camel's hair topcoat walked past and got into a green Cadillac parked behind me. The same Caddy I had seen before going into the hotel. All at once I knew he was tailing me. I could find the girl and Keefer in Dresden. I wanted to talk to my tail.

I gave the cabbie my office address. The Cadillac came behind us, far enough back to make me know he didn't want to be noticed. The taxi dropped me at my building. I went up.

My corridor was as dark and empty as usual. That was fine now. I ran into my office, turned on the light, and got my big old pistol. There was a janitor's closet near the stairs. I made it, left the door open a crack, as footsteps came up.

He passed like a shadow. I saw good shoulders, but he was two inches shorter than me. I slid out behind him. Sometimes I forget I have only one arm, but this time I had my gun for a club, at least. He heard me, and turned.

I had a glimpse of a high coat collar, a low hat brim, two dark eyes, and some very white teeth—and no more. He lunged at me without hesitation. I swung my heavy pistol for his skull—and hit nothing at all.

He was there, and then he wasn't. Something hit me in the belly. A hard fist in my face. I hit the wall with my back, swung my pistol at him again, and missed again. Two fists hit one-two in my belly, another landed solid on my jaw. He had three arms, at least. I thought how unfair that was as my chin was hit and I landed on the corridor floor on my face.

CHAPTER FIVE

He turned me over. I saw a face that was broad and olive-skinned. A gray homburg, gray coat—No! A camel coat . . .

"Fortune?"

He grew smaller and smaller like a mirage fading down a tunnel. His head became as small as a pin, and his thick body stretched up and up to touch the ceiling.

"Fortune?" he said. "It's John Andera. You okay?"

He slipped into focus, became normal size, and I saw that he was standing over me where I lay on the floor of the corridor. John Andera, not the man who had hit me—unless?

"A man tailed me," I said, my jaw stiff and heavy. "A little shorter than you, not as broad. Brown eyes, camel's hair topcoat. Know him?"

"No," John Andera said. "What did he want with you?"

"I was going to find that out by ambushing him."

Some ambush. I wondered if I was ever going to learn that even with two arms I'd never have been a fighter. My "victim" had been a fighter, maybe a real one, the way he had moved.

"Did Francesca know any ex-professional fighters?"

"I don't know," Andera said. "I came for a report."

I sat up. My left eye was puffed, my face hurt, and my belly ached. But it was all bruises—too fast to have done much damage. I had gone down, stunned, but not really out. I stood up. It could only have been minutes or less.

"You didn't see anyone coming out of here?" I said.

"No, no one," Andera said.

"Come on."

I went down the stairs as fast as I could on stiff legs with John Andera behind me. In the gray noon only a few people walked along my street. Andera stood beside me, and I saw the green Cadillac. It was double-parked across the street with its motor running.

"There!" I said to Andera.

I heard the three heavy shots as something slammed into my head and the street went black.

A pale green ceiling, and a chemical smell. The ceiling was supposed to be a dirty ivory, my corridor. Why did my corridor smell of chemicals? I was on the floor of my corridor, I'd been knocked there. I . . . but why was the corridor so soft, my hand sinking in when I pressed?

I *was* on the floor outside my office. I had to be, of course. The man in the green Cadillac had . . .

What slammed into my head?

Shots. I'd been shot!

The shadow bent over me, close. A face.

"Did you see anything, Dan? Who shot you?"

Captain Gazzo not John Andera looked down at me, very close, and he was standing up, so I was high off the floor. How could a man float off the floor on a soft cloud if he was still alive and . . .

"Dan? Did you get a look at who shot you?"

"No," my own voice said from somewhere.

"A guess?" Gazzo said.

"No."

The pale green ceiling was a hospital room. The antiseptic smell. A soft, high bed. Now I knew that, so some time must have passed. A lot of time, or a little?

"How bad am I?" I said to the ceiling.

A face appeared over me. Captain Gazzo—again or still?

"That was this morning," Gazzo said.

I must have asked him out loud. I hadn't thought I had.

"You're okay," Gazzo said. "One shot creased your skull good. Probably a forty-five. We found you out cold on the sidewalk. You've got a nice groove on your head, and a fair concussion. No real harm, you're full of dope. You were alone, Dan? You didn't see who shot?"

I hadn't seen who shot. The Cadillac, yes, but there were other green Cadillacs, and I hadn't seen where the shots had come from. Had I been alone? No, but yes. For now.

"I didn't see," I said. "I was alone."

"You're bruised up from something else, too."

"I was hit," I said. "Earlier. Small man, didn't know him. He hit good. I'm tired, Captain."

It was dark outside when I sat up. They told me it was still Saturday. Still? Then I'd lost Friday already. I managed to eat. John Andera came to see me after dinner. He was nervous and different. His face was neutral. The shock was gone, the stunned look, as if my shooting had steadied him. Or maybe it was only the way he reacted to action and real danger he could come to grips with.

"How are you?" he asked.

"Not bad. You weren't hit?"

"No. I didn't see who shot, I was down on the sidewalk."

"What about the green Cadillac?"

He shook his head. "I didn't notice a Cadillac. There wasn't one when I got up, when the police came."

I said, "Someone is scared of me. It means that Francesca wasn't killed by chance, or in some robbery. She was killed for a reason someone wants to stay hidden."

"But you don't know who," Andera said, "or what he wants to hide, so it's no use to me. What else did you find?"

I told him about Mayor Crawford and his political fights, what Celia Bazer had said about Francesca and men, and about the blond, Frank Keefer. "Keefer threw Celia Bazer over for Francesca in Dresden, then she threw him over. I don't think he'd have liked that. Did Francesca ever mention him?"

"No," Andera said. "She mentioned no one."

"She seems to have been pretty isolated down here," I said. "What did she talk about on your dates?"

"Us."

"Where did you meet her for your dates?"

"At restaurants. She didn't want me to come to her place. I never knew where she lived."

"No mention of a Harmon Dunstan or Carl Gans?"

"Do your women talk about other men on early dates?" Andera said. "Will you need more money, Fortune?"

"I'm covered for the hospital, mostly. I'll give you a bill. I'll probably go to Dresden. That means expenses."

"When you need them, tell me. I'll come back."

He left. I lay in the hospital bed feeling all my bruises, and the deep groove in my head hidden under a mound of gauze. Francesca Crawford hadn't died in a random killing, no.

I rested and slept all day Sunday. My concussion was gone, and my appetite was fine, and they would let me out on Monday. I was in no hurry. In the hospital I was safe. But I wouldn't fight to stay in after Monday. I was getting mad, and three days is a long time for a trail to grow cold.

Captain Gazzo came again after lunch on Monday. I was up in a chair, ready to dress when they told me. Gazzo took another chair, straddled it. I told him about what Celia Bazer had said, but not about Frank Keefer. I didn't want Keefer chased or picked up yet.

"We talked to Dunstan, Gans and the Emerald

Room," Gazzo said. "No help I can see. What about who shot you?"

"Nothing I can tell. I'd just tried to ambush a tail on me, got clobbered. I went down to the street, and wham," I said. "All I saw of the man tailing me was a camel coat, brown hat, green Cadillac, and fast fists. He may have been an ex-pro fighter the way he handled himself."

Gazzo shook his head. "Not enough to help. We've combed her neighborhood for anyone who might have seen anything, or for signs of anyone hanging around her place. Nothing we don't already know, no one saw the killer enter or leave."

"Celia Bazer says Francesca was in New York before she moved into the Eighty-fourth Street place."

"Sure," Gazzo said. "She came to town two months ago, took an apartment on Carmine Street. None of the tenants there seem connected to her. She went to that Harmon Dunstan for a job, but got Dunstan himself for a while instead. For two weeks she didn't work, just dated Dunstan. Then she took the job at the Emerald Room, began to see Carl Gans, and moved to the Bazer girl's place."

The captain rubbed his tender jaw. "Her job was below what she could have gotten. I can't see why she took it. She wasn't running in any kid crowd, she wasn't after a career, she was solitary but busy, and she told no one anything."

"No young men, no female friends except Bazer," I said. "Unusual. Not the standard young girl in the city for fame, fortune, or husband."

"Two men in two months, both old for her, and what do they have in common?" Gazzo said. "Dunstan is a businessman, Carl Gans is the bouncer at the Emerald Room. You tell me?"

"They're men," I said.

"And both have alibis, more or less."

So did my client, and he was a third man—also over forty. That was some pattern. Only I was sure that my client's alibi would hold up. That didn't make it a true alibi, but it did mean that Andera was sure no one could break it. And it looked like Gazzo hadn't turned up Andera yet.

"Without witnesses, or some solid evidence," Gazzo said, "nothing down here points to anyone, Dan. I've got Sergeant Jonas up in Dresden, but if he doesn't find anything we can use, we're stumped. The killer's a ghost."

"Maybe it was only bad luck in the big city."

"And the man who shot you is protecting the city," Gazzo said, leaned over his chair. "There's a missing month, you know? Between leaving Dresden, and coming here. I can't send a man without a lead, Dan, but you can tackle that. Do that for me, Dan. Find me that missing month."

I nodded. It wouldn't be easy to trace a hidden month in the life of a dead girl. The way she had stayed to herself, used a false name, we might never find where she'd been at all. While I thought about it, I realized that Gazzo was thinking, too. He was rubbing his face again, thoughtfully.

He said, "You know who owns the Emerald Room, Dan?"

"No."

"Abram Zaremba," Gazzo said. "Commissioner Zaremba to you and me. He had some state job once— Fish and Game Commission, I think. He likes to be called Commissioner."

I knew the man. Upstate, Abram Zaremba was a man to know. Whatever business you did, Zaremba could help. Power, money, and a lot of influence. No one said he was illegal, exactly, but he had a lot of "friends" who would do anything he wanted done. And Martin Crawford was a reformer, a crusader.

"I didn't know he operated in the city here."

"He has businesses here. He lives near Dresden, Dan."

"You've talked to Zaremba?"

"About a bar waitress with a phony name? I'd just warn him away, and a judge would talk to the chief. I know three judges who drink his booze every week. I'd need a reason."

"He wouldn't go to a judge about me," I said. "I can try a talk with Carl Gans, and look around."

Gazzo was silent for a time. He knew what chasing Abram Zaremba could mean, and it was no TV game. He sighed.

"You've got to be some use to me," he said.

A joke, but it really wasn't funny. I might smoke something out when a cop never could—because my Zaremba would be sure to try to stop fast if there was anything to smoke out. A cop might scare him to cover, but I wouldn't scare him. He'd know what to do with me. I'd been shot once already.

A detective captain has a hard job. Maybe I could help him, and it was his job to use me even if I ended up dead. It was my job, if I was going to do my work, to take the chance.

CHAPTER SIX

I left the hospital at two o'clock that Monday, too early for the Emerald Room. It was a momentary reprieve, and I took the Long Island Railroad out to Hempstead.

It's a suburban town a lot like thousands of small, busy, middle-class cities all across the country. It could be in Colorado, except for a total lack of natural beauty. There was only one Harmon Dunstan in the telephone book. I got a cab, and it took me to a large, pleasant brick house on a quiet street not far from Hofstra University. A flawless lawn surrounded the house under trees that were all but leafless now. An empty swimming pool was at the side next to a large patio under a green awning. There was a busy feel to the house, as if it was worked on a lot.

As I walked up the brick path, I was aware of eyes at the front window, and a slender blonde of about thirty-five opened the door. Her face had the residue of the too-perfect beauty you see in magazines, and her body was still good. She wore loose slacks and a dirty shirt as if she had been cleaning.

I said, "I'm looking for Mr. Harmon Dunstan."

"About what?"

"It's private. I'm a detective. You're Mrs. Dunstan?" She nodded. "Come in then."

So Harmon Dunstan was married. To a wife who wasn't surprised that a detective would call. I followed her into a big living room that was arranged and polished like a jewel. She headed for a home bar in a corner.

"A drink, Mr.—?"

40

"Dan Fortune. Too early for me, thanks."

I saw that she was a little drunk. Her blue-gray eyes had a film on them like thin plastic as she mixed herself a Bloody Mary. I heard the man behind me.

"Too early for anyone," the man said, but there was no anger in his voice, only a kind of concern. He held his hand out to me. "Harmon Dunstan, Mr. Fortune."

We shook hands. It was a hollow gesture, like the polite handshakes of enemy diplomats. He was about five-seven-or-eight, thin and dark-complexioned. Dressed all in gray, in a strangely old-fashioned way—gray fitted topcoat, gray business suit, gray gloves, gray tie, gray homburg, and black shoes, as if he had been about to go somewhere. The elegance of thirty years ago, as if he dressed in a style he had seen and wanted when he was a poor boy, and had never forgotten. Changes in fashion had not affected his dream.

"Can we talk in private?" I said.

The wife said, "He's a detective, Harmon," and she said to me, "I know about Francesca Crawford. Harmon told me."

Dunstan said, "I recognized her picture in the Thursday paper. I knew her as Fran Martin, of course. I told Grace."

"You went to the police?"

"No, I didn't. They came anyway," he said. "I had hoped it wouldn't come out, Fran and me. I'm a financial counselor, a delicate business. I can't have scandal, you see?"

But he had told his wife. Why?

"I have to ask some questions," I said.

He sat down, still in his topcoat, as if he'd forgotten he had it on. There was something peculiar about the way he moved. It was his eyes. They seemed to react to what he was doing only some seconds after he had moved. I sensed that he could sit unmoving for hours, and that his eyes never revealed what he was going to do until he had done it.

"I met Fran two months ago," he said unasked. "I took her out, bought her some clothes. It lasted five weeks, then she seemed to have no more time for me."

"When did you see her last?"

"After she moved, I went to Eighty-fourth Street a few times. She was always busy. The last time was a week ago."

"Why did she lose interest?"

"No explanation. I'd thought that if I tried harder—"

He didn't trail off, he just stopped, and I felt I was in some surrealist landscape. The shape of things was wrong. As if some trick had transported the Dunstans, the house, and me to an alien world where the familiar became weird. It was the way Harmon Dunstan was talking about himself and a young girl in front of his wife, a stranger, and the shiny furniture of an ordinary middle-class house. It was the way Grace Dunstan listened without anger, without any reaction at all.

I said, "You chased her after she lost interest?"

"I went to see her, yes. Perhaps, if she hadn't been—"

"Were you sleeping with her?"

He didn't answer. I guessed that he never would, and who could say now if he had or not? If there was any outside evidence of sex, I'd have to find it.

"Did you know she had other men?"

"I saw Carl Gans once. No one else."

"Not a John Andera?" I described Andera.

"No, but I wasn't spying on her, Fortune."

"Weren't you?" I said.

Something happened to his face. It went soft, loose, like a desperate boy in some hotel with an older woman. His face was coarser, almost fleshy, and he breathed faster. He blinked up at me, but he said nothing.

"How did you meet her, Dunstan?" I said.

"She applied for a job in my office. I didn't have a job for her, but we somehow started talking. She had just come to New York, knew no one. I asked her to have dinner. That's how it began. She seemed to like me at first, a lot."

Grace Dunstan said, "That's not an invitation Harmon would have missed or refused."

"Shut up, Grace!" Dunstan said.

The wife stared at him, but said no more. Somehow, I didn't think she was concerned with Dunstan's philandering at all. It was as if she wondered about Francesca's quick interest in Dunstan.

"You both have alibis for Tuesday night?" I said.

"We were both here at home all night, yes," Dunstan said.

It was no alibi, and yet as good as most. Normal for two innocent people to have only each other for an alibi. It would be true of most couples any given day or night. But it left them with no witnesses but themselves, and they sat there solid and together when I left.

I walked back to the station. I wanted to think—especially about the way Francesca Crawford had seemed to meet certain men. Casually, but not really so casual.

I carried my duffel coat on my arm when I walked into the Emerald Room this time, and went straight into the bar. I ordered a whisky, aware that I was being watched all the way.

The middleweight bouncer stood just inside the door. His suit hung loosely from his shoulders. He was all shoulders, narrow hips, no belly, and heavy thighs. His nose had been broken more than once. His blue eyes moved in slow sweeps around the restaurant. Despite his face, his manner was mild and inconspicuous, but nothing was going to happen that he didn't see almost before it happened.

He walked in small circles near the door, and each time he passed the telephone booths he paused to feel inside the coin returns. It was the habit of a simple, poor kid who had missed no chance for a lucky nickel to make life better. I saw a waiter walk up to the bouncer. Gans nodded, and came to me.

"You working on a case, Fortune?"

I knew what the waiter had said to him. They had run a check on me as I sat there—fast and sure. It made me feel like a worm in a garden with the boots of giants all around wherever I crawled.

"I came to talk to you," I said. "About Francesca Crawford."

"She said her name was Martin here," Gans said.

He looked over my shoulder, doing his job of watching the place. His voice was light and hoarse, but mild.

"A teaser? She made a play, but no action later?"

"She liked to talk a lot," he said dryly. "You working for the family? That mayor and all?"

"In a way."

"Funny, her being a mayor's daughter. I figured she was no waitress, but she did her job. Knew all about how to wait tables in a bar. Like she knew how inside, you know?"

"Some girls know that in their bones," I said.

"Yeh, like that," he said. "She knew how to handle herself, and no play, so I dropped her."

"She talked too much," I said. "About what?"

"Nothin' much. Shows, books, about how I used to fight for the Commissioner only I didn't have it to go higher than six-rounders so he put me here when we opened. I mean, I talked about that."

"You were a fighter? For Zaremba?"

"Commissioner," Gans said. "When I got my growth, had to move up to middleweight, I didn't have the punch. Good enough for a bouncer, but not for a real fighter."

He said it simply. I had the feeling that he was a simple man who had muscles to earn his living, and not much else, and that he knew it, and was grateful he had work at all.

"What else did she talk about?" I asked.

"Nothing," Gans said. "Just talk, you know? She—"

A small, balding man in a very expensive dinner jacket stood there. He was over sixty, his face round and owlish, and his eyes were small. A silent man stood behind him and watched only me.

"What does he want here, Carl?" the older man said.

"Asking about the Martin kid, Commissioner," Gans said. "I mean, Crawford. You know, the kid worked here a while and got killed last week?"

"Why would I remember a waitress?" Abram Zaremba said. "Why does this man come here about her?"

His voice was firm, but he'd just made a mistake. No one had mentioned that Francesca had been a waitress. Zaremba remembered her, knew about her.

"I took her out a couple of times," Carl Gans explained.

"So? You have an alibi, Carl?"

"I was here till two A.M.," Gans said. "I played cards with some of the guys past four A.M."

Abram Zaremba made it sound as if he'd never asked Gans about the alibi before, but that could have been an act for my benefit. The alibi could have been arranged by Zaremba, too.

"Then you're clear," Zaremba said, and turned to me. "What's your name?"

"Dan Fortune."

He looked me over. "Get out of here."

He walked away. I was left with Carl Gans.

"The Commissioner said get out," Gans said.

I got out.

CHAPTER SEVEN

I had done worse than get nowhere. Abram Zaremba knew who I was now, and I knew no more than when I had gone in the club.

The cold wind that had been scouring the city for weeks blew me to the Lexington Avenue subway. I rode downtown thinking that in upstate cities Abram Zaremba was a very big fish with a lot of interests. Carl Gans worked for him, and he owned the Emerald Room. Was there some connection to Zaremba in the pasts of Harmon Dunstan and John Andera?

It was early, but I was still weak, so I stopped in a diner on Seventh Avenue where the Monday special was pot roast. While I ate, and rested, I thought that nothing yet really connected Francesca to Abram Zaremba except that she had taken a job at the Emerald Room she had no real reason to take.

The good pot roast eased my aches, and I walked on to my office to call Captain Gazzo. I wanted to hear that he'd found a lead, any lead, that would keep me from having to go up to Dresden, but I didn't have much hope—the dead girl had done so *little* in New York. A runaway girl usually tries to do too much with her freedom. Francesca Crawford had been so isolated, so cryptic, that I couldn't help feeling that some unknown shape lurked unseen and murderous in the shadows.

It was an impression, no more, but it was there, and that was why I jumped two feet on the sidewalk in front of my office building when a real shadow moved close in a doorway. Someone came toward me from the doorway. A woman.

I had no gun, as usual, and I was tensed to run when I saw the ghost. She came into the light of a street lamp —long dark hair pulled back, a hawk nose, faintly slanted eyes, broad cheekbones, and dark brown eyes. Francesca Crawford!

"Mr. Fortune?"

While my nerves jumped, my brain told me that there were no ghosts, and if this was Francesca Crawford she was alive. Yet I knew she was dead. By now, buried in Dresden, New York.

"Miss Crawford?" I said.

"Yes. Can I . . . talk to you? Please?"

Francesca Crawford—except, of course, it wasn't. No, not quite. There were no ghosts, and Francesca was dead. There was a different "feel" to this girl. The same face, but with make-up, and proper, conservative clothes.

"Turn your head left," I said.

She had no scar under her right ear.

"Her sister," I said. "Twins."

"Felicia Crawford," she said. "I want to know—"

"Not on the street," I said. "My office in there."

She shivered, and it wasn't the wind. She didn't like the look of my dark, shabby building. Neither did I. It was too well known to people who followed me and had guns.

"Come along," I said, and took her arm.

She flinched like a deer at my touch, but she let me lead her. She was an identical twin, but the years had accentuated the differences not the identity. She dressed differently, seemed younger, but I sensed that the real difference was inside. Francesca, from what everyone said, had been tough, difficult, the rebel. This girl seemed soft, quiet, the "good" girl who did what she was expected to do. A little weak.

"How did you know about me, Miss Crawford?" I asked.

"Mother and Dad talked about you. They told Mr.

Sasser you were investigating the . . . murder. I want to help. I want to know what you know."

I remembered the name of Anthony Sasser from Mayor Crawford's biography in *Who's Who*—the businessman who headed the Dresden Crime Commission with the Mayor's partner, Carter Vance.

"Your parents sent you?" I said.

"No, I came on my own. I just left. Today."

We reached my apartment, and I steered her up the stairs before she saw that my home wasn't much better than my office. In my five cold rooms she stared as if she didn't believe anyone could live there. She didn't know how even the poor of urban America lived, so how could she, or anyone like her, have any conception of how the poor of the earth lived? The millions to whom my five rooms would be a palace, my income a fortune, and my hash-house meals food beyond their dreams?

"How about coffee?" I said. "Or something stronger?"

"Coffee, please," she said. "You live here?"

"It has advantages if you don't want money, comfort, or status," I said as I plugged in my coffee pot in the kitchen, and then went around lighting my gas radiators.

"Yes, I see," she said. "There are a lot of things on the other side of the iron curtain around the Crawford house."

It had the sound of a quote, not her own words.

"Who said it that way?" I asked. "Francesca?"

"Yes," she said, and there were tears in her voice.

I sat down facing her in the living room. She perched on the edge of a chair. I lit a cigarette.

"You were close to Francesca?"

"No one was close to Fran," she said, and there was self-accusation in the words. Her sister was dead, and they had not been close. "I suppose I was closer than anyone, but we didn't think the same about a lot of things."

"Closer than Frank Keefer?"

"I don't think she was really close to him at all. She laughed with me at him and his uncle with their big ideas. I think she just, well, wanted him for a time, you know?"

"His Uncle Joel? What big ideas?"

"Anything to make money without working. Joel Pender works for my father, a water inspector or something Dad hands out. Most of the time Joel seems to do favors for city officials. So does Frank Keefer when he isn't selling used cars."

"And Keefer hoped to marry Francesca?"

"Frank Keefer?" She seemed surprised, and then not so surprised. "Maybe he did, but she wouldn't have married him."

"What didn't you think alike about, Felicia?"

She sighed. I could hear the coffee perking in the kitchen. She shook her head sadly.

"Fran questioned everything I took for granted. Even as a little girl we never knew what she'd think or do. Dad said she wanted to be the ugly duckling. He always tried harder to understand her, be nice. It made me jealous sometimes."

Her voice was harsh—on herself. She had been jealous, and now her sister was gone. The ugly duckling who had made a display of her scar. A symbol of her difference, her isolation? Under the surface, of course, the duckling was a swan.

"How did Francesca get that scar?"

"An accident when we were around three. She used to cry about it when we were little, and later she had nightmares. When we were fourteen she started wearing her hair so the scar showed. She and Mother had a terrible fight. Fran said Mother had always treated her different, so she'd be different, and show her scar to everyone."

"Was it true? Your mother treated her differently?"

"In a way. Mother did pay more attention to Stefanie and young Martin, but it was just that they were so much younger. Stefanie's only fifteen now, and young Martin is twelve."

"You didn't feel neglected?"

She shrugged. "A little. I'm the halfway type."

In the kitchen, the coffee stopped perking. I went out to pour two mugs. When I brought them back, I gave her one, lit another cigarette, and sat down. The coffee was good.

"Why did you really come to me, Felicia?"

Her face was steady. "I want to know who hired you."

"No one hired me. I met Francesca, I liked her."

"Then I want to help! Mother and Dad are doing nothing!"

"The police are working. It's their job."

"I want to do more. Mother and Dad don't care!"

"No," I said. "It's not enough to bring you down here alone. You've got some reason to think I might know something specific about Francesca you want to know. What?"

She looked at my cigarette. I gave her one, lit it. She smoked awkwardly. She had not smoked much, and maybe it was the symbol of a change in her.

"Fran was excited three months ago, Mr. Fortune," she said. "Keyed up, eager about something in Dresden. Today, someone followed me to the station. I don't know who it was, but I think something is wrong in Dresden."

"What? Why was Francesca keyed up?"

She drank her coffee. "I'm not sure, but out in California at college we both got involved in politics and conservation. When we came home this summer, Fran joined the opposition to a big development project in Dresden. It's in a swamp out on Black Mountain Lake. We used to pick blackberries out there, the land never was worth anything. Now a man named Abram Zaremba owns it. He's planning a housing development out there, and the city is draining the land, building a highway right through it."

She glanced up. "Fran seemed to think that there was something bad about the project. At first, she just opposed draining the swamp, but a few weeks before she left home she told me that the whole scheme could be a fraud, a cheat."

"Did she give you a reason for her change?"

"A young lawyer named Mark Leland told her. He was investigating the project on his own. She talked with him a few times, and then . . . then he was killed, Mr. Fortune. Murdered in his car. Stabbed, just like Francesca! She was with him that night, and she saw the murderer, but not well enough to help the police. He wasn't caught."

She finished her coffee. "Fran was depressed, and angry, too. She said everyone was useless, no one was any good, and that she was finished with Dresden. She was very down, and when I asked her why, she said I wouldn't see it her way."

She looked up at me again. "Then, the very next day after she said she was going to finish with Dresden, and was so low, she suddenly was all excited again. It was strange, Mr. Fortune. Almost manic, you know? That day she vanished."

I waited, but that was it. "You have no idea what had happened, Felicia?"

"No," she said. "Fran talked to Grandfather Van Hoek that day, but he was very sick, you know, and she was going away. I wanted to ask him if he'd said anything special to Fran, but he got sicker when she left, and died a few days later. Mother and Dad were with him when he died, but they said he hadn't told them anything about Fran."

"You asked all her other friends if they said anything? Or knew anything?"

She nodded. "Fran didn't have many friends in Dresden. We'd been away in college, and the last two years Fran didn't even come home in the summer. She worked out there in California with field workers. That's when she started to dress so wild and strange, too."

She finished her cigarette, and looked for somewhere to put her coffee mug down. My coffee table was beside her, but she hesitated, as if she'd never seen a table where you could put down a mug without finding a coaster first.

"After she left," I said, "did you hear from her?"

She nodded. "Twice. She wrote to a friend Mother and Dad don't know, Muriel Roark, and enclosed notes for me. She told me not to tell anyone, and didn't give any return address, anyway. All she wrote was that she was fine, was finding out what was real, things like that."

"You don't know where she wrote from?"

"The second letter was from New York."

"Any names? What she was doing? Why she was in New York? Where she'd been that first month away from home?"

"No," she said, "nothing like that."

"No, damn it!" I swore, stood up. "You came down here because you know something. Enough to make you think I might have some answers you want. Tell me what you know."

She stood too. "I don't know anything."

"You said someone followed you. Don't try to chase down a killer alone. You'll only get hurt."

Her face was pale. "Just . . . tell me who hired you."

"I told you no one hired me."

"I . . . I don't believe you."

"All right," I said. "I can't let you risk your own life. You'll have to convince the police you don't know anything about Francesca."

I went to the telephone. Her hand went into her small handbag. The little, silver, .22-caliber automatic in her hand was like a toy. I have as much courage as most men, and the odds were 99–1 she wouldn't shoot, and better that she wouldn't even hit me. At least, those were the odds if she knew much about guns. I didn't think she knew much, and that scared me.

"Put it away," I said. "The police will help—"

"No!" she cried. "How do I know who you're really going to call? I don't know who you're working for or why!"

I reached for the receiver. "You call the police, then—"

The little pistol exploded with a toy bang. The bullet wasn't a toy. I don't know where it went. I froze.

"Stand . . . still," she said.

She picked up her coat, backed to my door, and went out. I didn't chase her for five minutes. Then I went down to the street. Up at the corner I saw a taxi pull away. I went back upstairs. It was just after 7 P.M. If I drove fast, I could be up in Dresden before nine-thirty.

I called John Andera at his office to get his home number. He was still in his office. I told him about Abram Zaremba and the land deal, and that I was going up to Dresden. I'd get my expenses later.

I packed my old pistol and some clothes in a bag, and went out to rent a car.

CHAPTER EIGHT

Dresden is a grimy city of a quarter million on the banks of the broad, shallow North Fork River some miles above its junction with the Delaware. Founded before the Revolution, its red-brick factories on the river date from the industrial boom before the Civil War, and were left behind by areas of better facilities and cheaper labor. Now highways and truck transportation have boomed Dresden again, but the cleaner light industry of today is spread around the city, no longer tied to the river.

The old factories, and the downtown residential areas, have been left to the poor, the old, and the black. The new skilled workers live out in the hills surrounding the city, and the managers live near the tops of the best hills. Where once it huddled around narrow streets near the river, the city now sprawled into what was farm and forest not long ago.

It was 9:30 P.M. when I turned off the Thruway. Golf courses, drive-in movies, roadhouses and shopping centers ringed the city along the county highway, and just inside the city line it curved around a large, dark lake. A wide, blacktop road led in toward the lake. I turned down it.

It ended at a fenced hunting lodge on the swampy south shore of the lake. Across the swamp I saw the high shadow of an earth dike between the swamp and the deep water of the lake proper, and near the lodge a mammoth pumping station was at work draining the swamp. A sign identified the station as property of The

Dept. of Public Works, City of Dresden, 9th Drainage District.

I lit a cigarette, and sat there for a moment before I drove back to the highway. There was nothing at all anywhere in the swamp but the single lodge.

Mayor Crawford's house was at the crest of one of the higher hills of the city. Vast green lawns surrounded large brick and stone houses distant behind iron gates and gravel drives to coachhouse garages. The Crawford house was one of the largest, in reserved Tudor style, set closer to the street than most because there were two cottages behind it. It had the dignity and quiet of long power, an old family.

The gates across the driveway were open, and I drove in. I parked in front of the house—and saw the green Cadillac. It was in front of the garage. I was sure it was the same Caddy my tail had driven in New York, and I stared at it. Someone was very careless, or very confident. I got out, and saw the woman inside a lighted, glassed-in side porch.

She looked out at the night like a lighthouse-keeper's daughter searching the sea for a lost lover. Her face turned, and I saw that it was Mrs. Katje Crawford. She acted as if she didn't really see me, or if she did I had no meaning for her. Her face was drawn and distant, like the face of a starving woman. Only it wasn't hunger, it was a kind of inner pain. I was seeing her private face, and it wasn't pretty. Her daughter was dead at twenty.

The front door opened as I walked toward it. A man came out—small, stocky, in a camel's hair topcoat but with no hat. Swarthy, he had sharp dark eyes and white teeth, and he was the man I'd "ambushed" tailing me in New York. I was certain. He had arrogant shoulders, walked with a confident strut, and the thin smile of his white teeth wasn't in his eyes. I doubted that his eyes ever smiled. A man with no time to waste on smiling for anything but show.

"You want something, Fortune?" he said.

I said, "You're one up on me. Should I guess?"

"Anthony Sasser," he said. "You must have done your homework in the hospital."

"After you put me there, Sasser?"

His dark face was full of contempt. "You want a confession? I didn't see who shot you any more than you did. Loused me up, too. I wanted to go on tailing you, but after you got hit, I had to get out. Don't like being around a target."

"That's your story."

"Prove it's not true."

"You tailed me, knocked me around."

"Sure. You jumped me, you had a gun. What do I do? You asked for it, and you got it."

"Why tail me?"

"The Crawfords asked me. You didn't know me, and they wanted to know who hired you. They've got a right."

"No one hired me, Sasser."

"That's your story," he said, mimicking me.

"You were a professional fighter once?"

"Me?" His eyes closed up. "Not me. Just a businessman."

"You never fought? I can check."

"Check," he said. "You won't find anything."

"Not even amateur? In the gym? Lessons?"

"I got better ways to have fun."

I was sure he had been trained as a fighter—sometime, somewhere. It's something a man can't hide. Yet he seemed just as sure I couldn't find out, as if his past was unknown. I thought about that as I looked toward the big house.

"You're at home here it looks like," I said.

"Old friend of the family," he said. "Business, too."

"Is the Mayor at home?"

His whole face stiffened. "No, at some meeting. You want the Mayor? I can drive ahead and show you where."

"Mrs. Crawford'll do for now," I said.

He didn't like that, me talking to Katje Crawford. "Be easy around Katje, Fortune. This is our city, my city. Don't lean too hard while you're nosing around without a client."

"I just want to help find who killed her daughter."

"Sure," Sasser said.

He walked past me to his Cadillac. Mrs. Katje Crawford was in the open doorway now. We both watched Sasser drive away. Then I walked to the door.

"Mr. Fortune, isn't it?" Katje Crawford said. "Come in."

She wore a long, flowing white robe that accentuated her drawn face and forty years. She looked older now, the strain on her handsome face, a rigidity in her athletic body. But she strode ahead of me through an elegant entry hall and across a living room like a public hall in some palace—but a lived-in room, too. Her dark blond hair swung to her stride, the hair too long for her age—a small vanity. We went out into the glassed side porch.

"Sit down," she said. "Will you have a drink?"

"Irish if you have it," I said.

She had it, and made the drink herself at a small bar in a corner. There had to be servants, but a patrician didn't ring for the maid to make one drink for a single guest. Even the porch furnishings were rich antiques in fine taste. It was a taste that comes only from growing up with fine pieces, living with them, appreciating them. I don't often feel like a peasant, but here I did. We're not used to that feeling in this country because we have so little real aristocracy, and even they are becoming more "common man" these days.

She brought my whisky. "Now. You'll say who hired you?"

"No one did," I said. "Is Felicia home yet?"

"Felicia?"

"She came to New York to see me. She had a gun. She ran. I think she's out to find the killer herself."

Her face almost collapsed. She stood and rang a bell. A maid appeared.

"Is Miss Felicia home?"

"No, ma'am. She left this afternoon, with a suitcase."

"Thank you, Paula."

The maid left. Katje Crawford's clenched hands told me that she wanted to ask a hundred more questions of the maid, but one didn't ask private questions of a maid. When she sat again, the lines of her face had deepened into dark slashes. She sat very still for a minute or more, spoke to herself:

"How many daughters must I lose?"

There was no answer to that. She didn't expect one. She listened to her own answers for a time. I drank my Irish.

"I think Felicia knows something we don't," I said.

She shook her head as if to clear a spell, and smiled at me apologetically, her silence rudeness to a guest. "I'm sorry, I'll be all right. Knows something? What could Felicia know? You mean about Francesca? She would have told us."

"Francesca wrote to her twice, Mrs. Crawford, asked her not to tell anyone."

"Francesca wrote? I see. You think something in a letter?" she said. "But Felicia would have told us— now."

"Maybe not. Felicia said that Francesca felt neglected, different, not loved. Felicia could be keeping faith."

Katje Crawford winced. She was a dynamic woman, and her thoughts were mirrored in her face, her active body. An energetic, sinuous body younger than her age, and I felt her as a woman. An attraction. That doesn't happen often to me on a case. But I was aware of

Katje Crawford, of her strength. Maybe there had been more of her in her daughter than Francesca had realized. Too much, maybe.

"Yes, it's true," she said. "My fault, but not all mine. Francesca was combative, what Tony Sasser calls a 'hardhead.' But I wasn't the mother to the twins I've tried to be to the younger ones. A young matron with her own interests and a rising husband makes a bad mother sometimes. Then, we just weren't close, not alike. A streak of isolation in the girls, even Felicia. Still, you can't blame the child. My guilt. What do I do now, Mr. Fortune? For Francesca, nothing. To catch who killed her won't give me any sense of achievement. But what do I do for Felicia? Where is she?"

"Help me find Francesca's murderer fast." I said.

She nodded. "Yes. What can I tell you?"

"What you know about Abram Zaremba and the Black Mountain Lake project."

"The project is a needed housing development. We're growing too fast. What else should I know?"

"Francesca worked against it?"

"She had strong ideas on ecology. Is it important?"

"What about Abram Zaremba?"

"I don't know him personally. My husband does, I think. Has all this some connection to Francesca?"

"Mark Leland had," I said. "You know about him?"

"Of course I do," she said, moved her lean hand in a sharp gesture. "We thought of that at once, Mr. Fortune, but Mark Leland was killed over three months ago. Francesca couldn't describe the man she saw running from Leland's car. Lieutenant Oster tried everything with her, she simply didn't see enough. Some hired killer, anonymous, the Lieutenant thinks. Far away by now. What danger was Francesca to him?"

"Maybe none, but Mark Leland was investigating the Black Mountain Lake project when he was killed."

She sat silent. Then she got up and went to an inlaid side table, a beautiful piece of work by some eighteenth-

century English craftsman. She took a cigarette from a
jade box, and lighted it without waiting for me to fumble
for my lighter.

"You think Francesca was killed because of that
development? A few thousand acres of swamp land!"

"She was involved with Mark Leland in more than
just seeing a man run from killing him. They'd met,
talked."

"Talked? Then tell Martin! Tell my husband, he
knows about that project. Find out, Mr. Fortune!"

She came back to her chair, and her legs seemed to
give way as she sat. "We have all we want or need, we
hurt no one by it, but she had to be militant. Look for
battles she was no part of. Man is a scheming animal,
that's what marks us, Mr. Fortune—we strive for ourselves. Perhaps it's wrong, and perhaps it will kill us
all, but it can't be changed."

The life in her face was animated even in despair and
anger. I could feel her presence all the way down my
back.

"There's another possibility in Dresden," I said.

"More?" She half-smiled. "You know your work,
don't you? Strange, one wouldn't guess it to look at
you."

"A one-armed roustabout?" I said.

She shook her head. "The one arm is incidental. It
gives you a piratical look, nothing more. No, it's your
dress and manner. You seem inconsequential, unedu-
cated, but you're not at all, are you? You know that my
side table is eighteenth-century English, and good. I saw
it in your eyes. People underestimate you, don't they?
They confuse a missing arm with a missing intelligence,
and I think you foster that image."

"It's just me, Mrs. Crawford."

"Perhaps," she smiled. "What is the other possibility?"

"Frank Keefer."

She nodded. "I know, but it was never serious. Francesca toyed with him, found him physically interesting.

I expect he had other thoughts, but he's a fool with grandiose ideas."

"She dumped him just before she left."

"Did she? I didn't know, but would that make him kill her? She was the golden girl he wanted. Why kill his dream?"

"Maybe because he couldn't have her?"

"Frank Keefer?" At another time she would have laughed. Now she only smiled. "He's the stupid, dull type who never gives up. To admit that a woman was beyond his grasp, would never have him, would lower his self-esteem so much I doubt if he could consider that possible."

"Would he kill to keep her?"

She hesitated. "I would say no, he hasn't the necessary moral strength, but I suppose you never can be sure. Anyway, it's Francesca who's dead, Mr. Fortune. How would that mean—"

"Maybe Keefer made a mistake," I said.

She was silent again. I stood up.

"If Felicia comes home, sit on her and call me, okay?"

The "if" seemed to weigh down the porch, but she nodded.

"Where can I find your husband now?" I asked.

"At a meeting of civic leaders at City Hall. He has to go to these meetings, but it's a terrible bore for me."

There was an annoyance on her face as I left, as if thinking of a lot of things that bored her.

CHAPTER NINE

City Hall was in an old, downtown section of Dresden. An ugly graystone building in late Victorian style. Floodlights bathed it in a glare, and the lawn was manicured in an attempt at some dignity.

The chill night, the big building in its square, and the dark, narrow streets leading off into a silent, deserted black made me think of London. I could almost feel the fog, hear the mellow musical sound of a London police whistle.

A night guard at a desk inside called up to the Mayor's office for me. Two silent black women mopped the lobby floors. It was dim and cold in the lobby, bare, as if designed to prove that the city fathers did not spend taxpayers' money on frivolous decoration. (We seem to insist that city employees work with none of the shine and comfort of private companies, but happily swallow the plush homes and privilege city leaders have in private life.)

I found the Mayor's office on the second floor where he waited for me alone now. It was a big, austere office, and Martin Crawford seemed smaller behind his desk. He also seemed tired. Maybe it was too much civic-minded meeting.

"You have some news, Mr. Fortune?" he asked.

He was the first one in Dresden who'd asked that, who hadn't been more concerned with who my client was.

"I'm sorry," I said. "We don't have much to work with."

He nodded. "The New York police sent a man here.

But where do you look for what killed a girl out in a jungle?"

"She'd left home before. Four years in college, even the summers away. She knew how to be alone on her own."

"College, even a big California farm, is a lot different from New York, Fortune."

"It is," I agreed. "Have you heard from Felicia?"

"Felicia?" he said, exactly as his wife had. They say people grow like each other in a long marriage. "What should I have heard from her? She's not mixed in this!"

I told him what I'd told Mrs. Crawford. "Whatever it is she knows, or thinks she does, she's scared enough to carry a gun and trust no one."

"But what? Something about Francesca?"

"I'd say so," I said. "Something Francesca told Felicia she wouldn't tell you or your wife. Your wife admits she was apart from the twins. Were you apart from them too?"

His blue eyes seemed to lose light, and his polished public face went loose like a man who is unsure. There was something about the way it happened that said it had happened before, often. A private face now that hinted at confusion, weakness, ineffectuality. As if his public manner was a façade, a front of confidence, and under it he was hollow and accustomed to having someone else make the real decisions that he carried out with his public smile and lawyer's eyes.

"I was busy, up in Albany so much," he said. "I left them to Katje. Then, later, it seemed too late. At least for Francesca. I leaned over backwards to get to know her. She never helped. Yet I think I loved the older girls best, in a way."

"Felicia could be in danger," I said bluntly. "Francesca was killed for a reason, and the killer won't take a chance on Felicia whether she knows anything or not as long as she's running around acting as if she does."

"What can I tell you?" Crawford said. "What do I know?"

"About Abram Zaremba and the Black Mountain Lake development," I said.

His manner changed as if a steel rod had gone up his spine. The impression of softness, indecision, vanished. Whatever gave him that aura of ineffectuality wasn't in his official work. The lawyer faced me now.

"What concern is that to you?" he snapped.

"It concerned Francesca, right? She fought it?"

"Conservationists! A bunch of juveniles and old women who don't have any idea of reality. A mayor has many things to consider, Fortune. It was my opinion that the benefits to the city, the desperate need for housing, outweighed the ecological factors. That was my decision, and it stands unless the people throw me out, which is their right."

Before he finished his speech, a door to the left opened, and Anthony Sasser stepped quietly into the room. The businessman got around. I wondered if he'd been listening all along in an adjacent office. He moved with ease, a man in his own backyard. He sat down to my left, silent and alert. I ignored him, faced Crawford.

"Who else objected to the project besides conservationists?" I said. "Maybe the taxpayers? Or maybe they would object if they knew how the deal was arranged? You built a dike at public expense, maybe paid Zaremba even for the land you built the dike on? You put a nice road into Zaremba's lodge. You created a drainage district so the taxpayers can buy bonds, the taxpayers foot the whole drainage bill? Drainage that will make useless land a goldmine?"

"It's a proper arrangement under our conditions," Crawford said. "Land is limited here. Zaremba's land, when reclaimed, will benefit the whole community."

"But first it benefits Abram Zaremba—a lot," I said.

Anthony Sasser spoke from my left. "Abram Zaremba is a businessman, he made a smart investment. It's all legal."

"You in on the project?" I asked Sasser.

"I wish I was," Sasser said. "It's a good deal for everyone. Marty there is right."

"Mark Leland didn't think it was a good deal for everyone, did he?" I said.

Sasser tilted his chair back and rocked in the quiet office. I had a feeling that I had just started walking on eggshells. Mayor Crawford's voice was low and smooth. The lawyer addressing a jury he wanted to impress with his gravity, but firmly set straight at the same time.

"How do you know that, Fortune?" the big Mayor said. "The police here don't know what Leland was doing in Dresden. We found no documents, and his lone partner doesn't even know what Leland was really doing. If you have information about Leland, you should tell our police and Crime Commission."

"You don't know he was investigating the Black Mountain Lake project?" I said.

"No," Crawford said, "we don't. Why would he? There's nothing to investigate. How do you think you know?"

"Leland talked to Francesca about it. Didn't she tell you?"

"No, she didn't," Crawford said, "not a word."

"She told Felicia."

Sasser said, "Hearsay. Maybe Felicia got it wrong. My Crime Commission found no evidence of what Leland was doing, and nothing wrong with the project. I'm not in the project, but I've worked a lot with Commissioner Zaremba, and I'd be careful about accusing him or the city government."

His voice was matter-of-fact, but I heard the warning in it. So did Martin Crawford. His lawyer manner slipped into a smile, man-to-man, smoothing the ruffled waters.

"There are always nuts who think every public deal has to be crooked, Fortune," he said, friendly. "They smell a shady deal when there isn't one. It's a way to get a reputation with the public. You get used to that in government."

"This nut was dangerous enough to someone to be killed," I said. "Someone thought there was trouble around."

Anthony Sasser said, "No one knows why Leland got killed. Maybe he got in trouble someplace else."

"A coincidence he was killed here, and that Francesca saw the killer, and now she's dead?"

Crawford said, "The police, and Tony there, questioned her carefully, showed her every mug book. All she saw was a man running, her identification was useless."

"Maybe she saw more than she said, or someone thought she had," I said. "You seem pretty anxious to think Francesca wasn't mixed up in the project."

Crawford let a silence stretch for a time as if he were thinking about Francesca and the project—a daughter and an important political situation.

"I back the project, Fortune," he said slowly. "We need the housing, that land is the best we can get. I must follow my judgment. It's a normal, legal business arrangement."

"Maybe that's what's wrong with it—it's legal, but not exactly ethical or moral," I said.

"If you can find anything legally unethical," Crawford snapped, "I'll kill the project myself."

"You're a good lawyer, and Abram Zaremba probably has better lawyers," I said. "It'll be legal as hell, but there are legal deals that aren't so moral. Favors, collusion, private arrangements that never show, little tricks of dealing. I've known legal deals that sent citizens for their guns when they figured out how they were getting fleeced. That drainage district, for instance. I'll bet the only land in it is that swamp of Zaremba's. A neat way of making the public foot the bill for draining one man's land."

Crawford said, "The city, in my judgment, needs the project. Inducements are often necessary to entice a private businessman to help the city."

Sasser said, "Every public project benefits someone in our country, Fortune. You can't build a sandbox without using someone's land and paying him for it. A man has a right to make money on his property."

"It looks like Mark Leland didn't think so."

Sasser said, "Maybe Leland was a crook out for himself. Blackmail to get cut in. A guy like that could ruin a good project, and that could make some people awful mad."

"That justifies murder, Sasser?" I said.

"No, but maybe it explains it," Sasser said softly.

They both sat like impassive Buddhas in the quiet office. Were they telling me something? Had Mark Leland been out to make a nuisance of himself, stir up doubts, in the hope of being bought off? It had happened before.

I said, "Tell me about Joel Pender. He works for you?"

"Pender?" Crawford said, surprised. "He's a minor employee, useful for small jobs, yes."

"He's worked for the city quite a while?"

"Eighteen years, yes. He's useful, sort of an errand boy. He's good at that kind of thing, reliable."

"Would he like to be part of your family?"

"My family? How the devil—"

Sasser said, "He means Francesca and Frank Keefer. You know, Marty, Keefer was making a big play for Fran."

Crawford watched me. "You think Keefer, or Joel Pender, might have killed her? That's crazy, no."

"Keefer was in New York when it happened, she'd

dropped him just before she vanished. Pender had a fight with her. I'll bet she could make people pretty mad, right?"

"She had a sharp tongue," Crawford admitted. "But if Keefer wanted her, why would he—"

"Men lose their heads over women. Or maybe make mistakes."

"Then find out, Fortune!" Crawford said.

Sasser said, "What makes you think the motive has to be up here, Fortune? She was gone three months. A wild kid."

"She was excited by something here before she left, and she'd been involved with Mark Leland and the housing project."

Martin Crawford leaned across his desk at me. "Listen, Fortune. We don't know why Mark Leland was killed, but it's clear that whatever the reason was it ended with Leland. Three months have passed with no trace of the killer. Leland had a partner, George Tabor. No one has touched Tabor. If Francesca or Tabor had known anything, do you think the killer would have waited three months, let them walk around to talk to almost anyone in that time? No. Do you think I'd cover anything that had led to the murder of my daughter? Do you?"

I said, "I don't know what you'd do."

They both just looked at me.

CHAPTER TEN

I checked into a motel not far from Black Mountain Lake. George Tabor was listed in the telephone book. I called from my room, late as it was, and he answered. I told him my name, and that I wanted to talk to him about Mark Leland. He had a flat, colorless voice.

"There's nothing I know," he said. "I told the police."

"It's two murders now, Tabor," I said. "Your partner had talked to Francesca Crawford, now she's dead. I want to know what he was doing with her."

"Using her," Tabor's blank voice said. "The way he used everyone else."

"I still want to talk to you," I said.

He breathed slowly on the other end. "All right. Come over," and he gave me the address.

I got my old pistol from my bag. Tabor had been close to Mark Leland. I drove to the address. It was a large park of garden apartments in a new suburb. A place for professional men, junior executives on the way up, and middle-aged businessmen who were as high as they would go. Tabor lived in the second building, third floor. He met me at his door.

He was a tall, thin man with the unsure eyes of a door-to-door salesman who wasn't doing well. He walked me inside without speaking. The television set was on to a football game. A can of beer stood on a table beside an easy chair. Tabor sat down in the easy chair, his eyes fixed toward the TV set. He waved me to a seat. I sat down.

"The Jets are ahead," Tabor said. "Fourth quarter."

On the TV the quarterback completed a long pass.

Tabor sipped his beer, leaned forward to watch the dark-shirted defenders swarm down the white-shirted receiver.

I said, "You worked with Leland on the Black Mountain Lake project? Investigating it?"

"I don't know what Mark was working on," he said. "Damn!"

The damn was for an interception on the TV. The Jets had been stopped. Tabor watched the teams change.

"His partner?" I said. "And you don't know his work?"

"We need linebackers," Tabor said as the enemy gained five yards up center on the TV. "Mark wanted publicity, had ideas of running for office. He was working on his own."

"Not working for any client? Any group?"

There was time out on the screen, but Tabor continued to watch. "No," he said.

"You know that much? Negative, but nothing positive?"

"Mark didn't tell me what he was doing, or what he'd found if anything," Tabor said, drank his beer, watched the TV screen where the Jets had the ball now.

"Why did he go to Francesca Crawford?"

"I don't know he did," Tabor said, moved forward in his chair as the Jets acted. "Look at that! What a catch! Go, go, go! He's loose! He . . . damn! It's okay, we'll score soon."

I said, "You can't help me at all?"

"There! Off-tackle, right, right—" Eager in his chair, battling through the line with the ball carrier. "I'm in all private practice now. Corporation stuff. No politics."

"Leland's work dropped? That was fast."

"Touchdown!" Tabor cried, turned to me with glittering eyes. I didn't even look at the screen. His eyes looked away. "I'm no hero, Mr. Fortune. Mark is dead, buried."

"Dead and forgotten?"

Tabor watched the kickoff on the screen. Behind us the outer door opened. Tabor didn't turn. I had heard no key in the door lock, it had been left open. I turned. Abram Zaremba stood in the room, the door shut behind him. He was alone.

"Out," Abram Zaremba said.

He wasn't talking to me. George Tabor went to a closet, got a coat, and walked out of his apartment. Zaremba went to the TV set and turned it off.

"Jets win by two touchdowns," he said, sat down facing me. "Who are you working for, Fortune?"

"So you got to Tabor? Gave him some business work?"

"I got to Tabor," he said. "Now I get to you. How much?"

"For what?"

"For your client's name, and for walking away."

"I don't have a client. I liked Francesca Crawford."

"You never met the girl until a morgue slab."

"If you know that, you know what she was doing in New York. You knew who she was, all about her. You were watching her."

"I watch what concerns my business."

"Like Mark Leland, Zaremba?"

"Commissioner to you," he said. "Don't talk too much."

He leaned, and slapped me across the mouth. I jumped up, my one fist balled, ready to hit him. An automatic response. But I didn't hit him. I just stood there. He was smiling.

"You want to hit me, Fortune?" he said. "Go ahead. Look, I don't carry a weapon," and he opened his elegant suit coat to show me. "I'm alone, right? Sure, I am. Go ahead."

I didn't move. Suddenly, there seemed to be doors all around me, open windows, other rooms where his men could be hidden and watching. My neck crawled. He almost purred, he was so pleased with himself, with his power.

"I'm no match for you, even with that one arm. You've got a gun in your pocket, right? What's stopping you? Go on, take a chance, maybe I'm really alone. No one around."

I was sure he was alone, but could I take the chance? No. His men could be behind any door, at any window. It's how men like him win—the fear of what they might do, can do.

I said, "You don't want me dead. Not yet."

"That would be stupid," he nodded. "But better silent and dead, than silent and alive to talk to someone else."

"A warning, Zaremba?" I said, my throat very dry.

"I don't warn," he said, disgusted with me. "If one means business, a warning simply alerts the enemy. If one doesn't mean business, the warning rarely has the desired effect. Men who are dangerous enough to need a warning rather than just a suggestion are usually much too intent on what they want to heed a warning. No, action counts, warnings dissipate force. If I intend to strike, Fortune, I don't warn. I'm not warning you, I'm simply offering to pay for information. What I'll do if you refuse, I haven't considered yet. It would depend on what you really know, and that's hard to assess."

There was just enough cold calculation in the speech to make me shiver inside. Menace without threat—the possible dangers left for me to consider. Up to me to decide where the balance lay. Was he stating his case openly, or bluffing me?

"You won't hurt me, not when I might know something," I said. "That's logical."

He sighed at me. "Logical? Rational? I make my living because people are rarely rational, Fortune, or logical. What people think is rational is only making what they need to do and to seem right and true. Ever see the man who is furious at the way the Commies send writers to jail when the writers do what the Commies don't like, turn around and favor censoring all writers who don't agree with him, picket un-American movies? Are you any better? Am I? No. Maybe I know what's logical, but maybe my private irrationality makes me act against logic."

"You should have gone into politics."

"It's easier to buy politicians. Do I get the name?"

"Maybe, if I get something, and not money," I said. "You knew Francesca Crawford was in New York. She was making plays for older men. Did she make a play for you, Zaremba? Did you tell her too much about something? Or did you like her, and after teasing you she turned you down?"

"Don't play guessing games, Fortune."

"Maybe you killed Mark Leland, or knew who did, and Francesca knew that?"

He moved in his chair, restless, as if making up his mind about me. Reluctant to decide. But decide what?

"I'll level, Fortune, this once. I've got a feeling that someone is using me. A private matter, okay?"

"Used you to kill Francesca?" I said.

He watched my face. "You know, I wonder if you do know anything? If you have a client after all? You're pretty free with the accusations, maybe shooting wild, hoping for a hit."

"But you don't know, and until you do, you won't do anything to me, will you? No, you couldn't. You're stumped."

"Are you so sure?" he said.

"I'm sure," I said. I could bluff too.

"Then let's have a drink, and talk man-to-man, okay?"

He went into Tabor's kitchen, out of my sight. When he came back he had a bottle of cognac and two snifters. He poured the brandy where I could see him, but he had the glasses hidden in his fleshy hands. I couldn't see if anything had been in the glasses before he poured.

Smiling, he handed me a glass. I looked at the dark brown liquid, the pungent smell of brandy hiding almost any other odor.

"Drink up, Fortune," Zaremba said, still smiling.

He knew what he was doing. Anything could be in my glass. If I refused to drink, his men could be in the room in seconds—if there were any of his men hidden and watching. I had to hope that I was right, that he was bluffing, putting a subtle pressure on me. I drank.

"You're a brave man," he said.

There was a taste to the brandy.

"Just relax," he said, purred. "You'll be fine soon. I really have to be sure, you see?"

I sat, and his face slowly began to dissolve like molten liquid. He became hazy. I tried to stand. I fell over. I was on the floor. I knew he was bluffing. Just a . . . drug.

I knew he was . . . bluffing.

. . . I knew . . .

CHAPTER ELEVEN

I opened my eyes. There was muted light. Not in the room where I lay, in some other room. I had a headache.

A headache!

I was alive. It had been only a drug. Alive!

Drugged, why? To take me somewhere, of course. So where was I? I looked at my watch. Eleven o'clock? The darkness said it was night, so unless I'd been out over twenty-four hours, less than an hour had passed. Then I couldn't have been moved far. I sat up.

I hadn't been moved at all. The same TV set seemed to watch me like a Cyclops's eye. The same room, Abram Zaremba smiling at me from the same chair but with the lights out. The only light was from the kitchen. I stood up, swaying on rubber legs.

"Okay," I said to Zaremba, "you slipped me a knockout. Why? To prove you could kill me if you wanted to?"

I think I hated Abram Zaremba at that moment as much as I had ever hated any man. The way he sat watching me shake with the effects of his power. He enjoyed it—making a man less than a man. There is nothing slimier on earth than one man making another less than a man out of very human fear. Fear is in all of us, can be used against all of us, and no one should enjoy that fear in another.

"Goddamn you, Zaremba," I said. "You hear me?"

He just smiled—and I saw the blood.

I swayed against a table. His white shirt was dark with blood in the dim light. He didn't hear me, no. He didn't hear anything. Zaremba was dead. In that chair, bloody and dead with a rigid death smile.

I held onto the table. I breathed to clear the drug from my head, and stepped closer. I touched him. He was still limp. Less than half an hour. The blood had dripped from his chest onto the floor under the chair, and had dripped nowhere else. Someone he had known then? Killed in that chair facing his killer, unaware of the danger?

With me lying drugged on the floor not ten feet away? The killer unconcerned about me? Or maybe very concerned, hoping I'd be accused of Zaremba's murder?

I began to search around the room, the floor, the furniture. My legs were steady now, the adrenalin pumping inside me. I found nothing that meant anything to me. No trace of blood, not a book out of place. There was nothing to do now but call the police. My hand was on the receiver when I heard the footsteps outside, and a key turned in the door. I had my gun out when George Tabor walked in. He stopped, blinked.

"Fortune? You're still—"

"You expected me to be somewhere else by now?" I said.

Tabor stood in his coat. "Zaremba said he'd take you with him somewhere, talk to you."

"Did you ask how he planned to 'talk' to me?"

"No," he said.

He didn't seem to care about my pistol. Still in his coat, he walked to the television set, turned it on, like a lemming obsessed only by the sea somewhere ahead. As if his whole consciousness was bound by the TV set and the simple world on the small, gray screen. No disappointments, no traumas, nothing to have to depend on for joy or happiness but the TV—a friend and lover that wouldn't let him down.

I said, "You must have been awfully afraid of Zaremba."

"Very afraid," he said, his eyes on his safe images on the screen. "I'm a sane man. I—"

My words must have suddenly struck him, the tense —"You must *have been* awfully afraid . . ." He turned, stared around the room, aware that I wasn't supposed to be here, and that if I was . . . He saw Abram Zaremba dead in the chair.

"You killed him?" he said. "You killed—"

"No," I said. "I had no reason. I want answers, and dead men don't help me. I might have defended myself, but Zaremba had no weapon, he must have been alone. But you were scared of him, and you just used your key to get in. You must have locked the door again when you went out, so who else could have come in and killed him except you, Tabor?"

"Me?" He still stared at the dead and bloody Zaremba as if afraid the dead man would rise up and hurt him. "Locked? The door? I don't know. Did I lock it? I—"

He stopped, blinked again as if my words were taking minutes to reach his brain. "Me? I didn't kill him! I just came back! I wasn't here!"

"Back from where?"

"Where? Walking. A drink. I stopped for a drink. Some tavern. I don't remember which one. A few blocks."

I said, "You had to know more about Mark Leland and what he was doing than you say you do. Zaremba believed you knew more or he wouldn't have paid you off. But men like Zaremba know that a more permanent solution is better than a payoff in the end, and maybe you guessed that, too."

Tabor stared at the dead businessman, and then at his TV screen where some smiling man was giving violent news. There was a longing in his eyes for the haven of the TV. The haven of a man whom life has burned, whose woman is asleep alone in the bedroom indifferent to him and without passion for him, whose friends have been buried. The TV is better than brooding in some dark corner and going insane with fear, or love, or despair. A peaceful illusion of reality.

"You better talk to me," I said. "Unless you want to wait for Zaremba's 'friends' who might think what I think."

Tabor collapsed inside, and came to life at the same time. He sat down, his back to the TV. Zaremba had had a lot of bad friends, and Tabor shivered. He had been afraid of Zaremba, and he was more afraid of Zaremba's friends. Sometimes fear brings a man to life better than joy or love.

"I didn't kill him, Fortune. I swear it. He gave me his word, I was no danger to him. I knew that Mark was investigating Black Mountain Lake, but he hadn't gotten anywhere as far as I knew. It was all legal. Mark said that it favored Zaremba, and smelled, and if he could stir up enough trouble, maybe Albany would have to suspend it, start a real investigation. But that was all he had. *Maybe* he could rock the boat enough to get the project suspended."

"Why did he go to Francesca Crawford?"

"She was Mayor Crawford's daughter, Mark smelled good publicity in her. She already opposed the project. He was going to try to show her that her father was at least unethical in the deal. And he knew something from Crawford's past, some legal shadiness, he hoped to use to make the girl help him by working against her father from inside."

"What did he know from Crawford's past?"

"I don't know. Neither did he, not for sure. Just a hint that Crawford had hidden something in the past."

I said, "Let me see your hands."

There was no blood on them, and they were grimy, unwashed. There was no blood on his clothes. Still, it didn't prove much.

"You just walked around, stopped for a drink?"

Tabor nodded. "Then I came back and waited down outside for a while. You or Zaremba didn't come out. No one came out, except . . . A woman," he looked up at me from his chair. "A woman came out about ten minutes before I came up. I didn't see much—just a woman, a tweed coat, maybe young. She walked off fast, with a swing, you know? A young walk . . . maybe."

A woman, maybe young. Athletic. Or who seemed young. Felicia? Celia Bazer? They were young. Katje Crawford? Mrs. Grace Dunstan? They could look young in the dark.

I went to the telephone now and called the police. With Tabor here, I couldn't just walk away this time, no. I gave the police my name, the address, and told them Abram Zaremba had been murdered. They would come fast. I hung up.

George Tabor was back at his TV set. He still had his coat on, but he wasn't in the room now. He was on the screen with some tall cowboy riding into a western town just after the Civil War. I joined him in that safe, distant town.

CHAPTER TWELVE

I sat alone, fighting sleep from Zaremba's drug, in the office of Lieutenant Oster, Dresden Police Homicide Division. I had been there since they'd brought me and Tabor in from the apartment. It was past 1:00 A.M. before Lieutenant Oster, and Sergeant Jonas from the New York police, got back to me. Oster sat behind his desk, Jonas leaned on a wall.

"Let's hear your story again," Lieutenant Oster said.

I told him. "Whoever killed Zaremba thought I was dead, or didn't care about me."

"Or maybe your story is all phony," Oster said.

Jonas said, "No knife in the apartment, Lieutenant."

"Knives can be dumped," Oster said.

"Zaremba was stabbed?" I said, my brain fuzzy.

Oster nodded. "Once in the heart. M.E. says he died instantly, a good hit. Never got out of that chair."

"The same M.O. as Francesca Crawford," I said.

Oster said, "You were alone with Zaremba."

"What's my motive?"

"Fear could be enough," Oster said. "We don't know you up here. Maybe you're working for the killer. Who's the client?"

I'd promised to let John Andera know before I named him, but if we could keep all our promises this would be a different world. I had no way of knowing if Andera had an alibi this time. I'd gone as far as I could go in protecting him.

"His name's John Andera, a sales representative for Marvel Office Equipment in New York. All I have is his office number."

I gave them Andera's number, and Sergeant Jonas got on the telephone to New York. I told Oster what Andera had told me as his reason for hiring me—just a man who'd liked a girl. Oster thought about it.

"Tabor's sticking to his story," he said. "You have any ideas about that woman he says he saw?"

My stump had that gnawing pain. Maybe it was only the effects of the drug, or maybe it was that uneasy feeling I have when I'm thinking what I don't want to think.

"Felicia Crawford," I said, and told Oster about her coming to me in New York. "Maybe she's back in Dresden on her own."

"She had a gun? No one reported her missing," he said. "Why would she kill Abram Zaremba?"

"Maybe she thought, or knew, that he killed Francesca."

Jonas came back and leaned against his wall again. My client was being checked on now in New York.

"Oh," I said, "there's Celia Bazer. She and Francesca were mixed with the same man. Women have killed each other for that before. Or men have had to eliminate one of the two women. Maybe Zaremba just knew who had killed Francesca, and was putting on some pressure."

"What man were they both mixed with?" Oster asked.

"Frank Keefer."

"We'll check," Oster said. "Anyone else, Fortune?"

"Mrs. Katje Crawford. Her daughter was killed."

"We're back to maybe Zaremba killed Francesca Crawford?"

"He was knifed for some reason, Lieutenant," I said.

"Okay, I'll work on all three women," Oster said.

"Make it four," I said, glanced at Sergeant Jonas. "There's a Mrs. Grace Dunstan in New York. I can't tie her to Zaremba, but she was tied to Francesca Crawford."

Jonas went back to the telephone. Oster closed his eyes.

"George Tabor isn't anxious to get turned loose, either," Oster said. "He seems happy in jail. Safe."

"Zaremba wasn't nobody," I said. "If I even might have killed Zaremba, I'd be scared. Mark Leland was his partner, and Leland was trying to wreck a big deal of Zaremba's."

"That project is all legal," Oster said. "In three months we've found no tie between Leland and Commissioner Zaremba."

"Zaremba fixed that," I said. "But you know."

"I work here, Fortune," Oster said. "The Mayor pays my salary. I investigate crimes, not public business."

"You like your job?"

"I have for fifteen years."

"What's your verdict on Mark Leland?"

"A man looking for a political edge. Digging for dirt. There's two sides to any business, Leland may have had his side, but I don't know why he was killed. A man like that makes a lot of enemies. We're investigating his private life."

"Muggers too? Investigating transients?"

"That's right, standard procedure. Leland was stabbed on a public street in his car, his wallet was missing. We may never solve it, or maybe some hobo shows up with the wallet."

"There was a witness."

Oster shook his head. "Francesca Crawford's description could fit ten thousand men. She picked no one from any mug book. She had no information on Leland except rumor. We followed every lead she gave us. Tabor knew nothing, Zaremba had an alibi, and the project is all okay."

"So Francesca was no danger to anyone?"

"Not that we can see. She knew nothing important, and it's been over three months. Who would be afraid of her?"

It was what had been said before—and it was solid. If Francesca had been a danger, the killer wouldn't have waited three months to silence her. Whatever she might have known, she would have told everyone by then. Unless she had kept something back, and the killer had just learned that. It was a slim possibility. Why would she keep anything back?

"Zaremba was eager to know who hired me," I said. "It's possible he just knew who killed Francesca. No connection to Leland and the project."

Jonas returned from the telephone. "You mean maybe he was protecting someone? Or blackmailing? What about that Anthony Sasser? He spends a lot of time around the Crawfords, he knew the girl, and he works with Zaremba. Not on the Black Mountain Lake project, but Sasser worked with Zaremba on other business."

"Sasser killed Francesca?" Oster said. "Christ, Jonas, Tony Sasser is like an uncle to those girls. What reason?"

I said, "Francesca's grandfather talked to her before she left town. How did the grandfather happen to die, Oster?"

"In bed, natural causes," Oster snapped. "Emil Van Hoek was eighty-two, had a bad heart and emphysema. He was about to die for years. Don't come here and beat bushes for straws!"

"We've got three stabbings, and a natural death," I said. "They have to be connected. If not by business, then somewhere in their private lives. That includes the grandfather."

Sergeant Jonas said, "Trouble in Zaremba's organization?"

"A business organization, not a gang," Oster said.

"Business that was always legal?" I said.

"As far as I know. Legal here," Oster said. "Okay, a man like Zaremba is killed, you have to think of a power play, a business battle, but this hasn't got the feel.

Simple murder with Fortune left alive. It's crude, messy, too open. No plan to it, and if it had been business there would have been a neat, careful plan."

He was a better cop than he had seemed. As good as his job allowed in a small city where pressure and influence were the way men lived. And he was right.

"Hate," I said, "not greed. A witness didn't matter."

"It looks private," Sergeant Jonas agreed.

"Everyone has a private life," I said.

We were all thinking about that when Oster's telephone rang. It was New York for Sergeant Jonas. He didn't talk for long. When he returned this time, he sat down.

"The Dunstan woman is out of New York," Jonas told us. "Her husband says she's visiting relatives in New Haven. He just got home himself maybe half an hour ago. We haven't found your client, Dan, he's not at his home. His office says he's in Philadelphia on business. We had to roust the office manager out of bed to talk, and he says Andera isn't due to call and report until tomorrow morning. His place is staked out."

There was nothing more I could do now, and I was close to passing out again. I left Lieutenant Oster and Jonas sitting in silence, and went down to my car. I drove to my motel, and fell onto the bed.

CHAPTER THIRTEEN

In drugged sleep I dreamed of running down a long tunnel after my missing arm that floated always ahead of me, mocking me to be a whole man again.

I woke to a gray morning heavy with a feel of rain coming, and the scent of pine needles outside. I reached for a cigarette. Abram Zaremba had given me the dream. I had let him slap me without hitting back because his men might have been around. I had meekly drunk the brandy trusting to my brain that told me it wasn't poisoned, instead of throwing it into his face because no man should ever crawl like that. If it had been poison, I'd have drunk my death for fear of possible death that just might be there in his hidden men.

Now I lay with the drug boiled out of me like the venom of a snake bite. Abram Zaremba had bitten me, and for a time I would feel that more was missing than my arm, but it would pass, a man goes on living with himself somehow. Zaremba, at least, would bite no one else with his moral poison, make no one else crawl to his power. In the end I had won—I was alive. But who had bitten the snake? It could have been anyone he had ever dealt with, but, like Oster, I had the feeling that this had not been any power murder, any "business" play. Zaremba had come alone to me in his arrogance. He had died alone without his "help" near him, his death as much a surprise to him as to everyone else. He had not expected danger, or he would not have come alone. If he had been in a power fight, that he would have known and come protected.

Unless he had not come alone, and one of his own

men had killed him. That was not uncommon in his world. But, again, that would have been carefully planned, and there was something unplanned about last night's murder.

Then, of course, it could have been George Tabor.

I heaved myself out of bed and went into the shower. I stayed under the hot water a long time. Partly to ease the pains from my bruises, and partly because I didn't really want to start looking again. George Tabor said he had seen a woman, maybe young, and Felicia Crawford was somewhere. I didn't want to track down Felicia if she had killed the man who had murdered her sister. But until I did find her I wouldn't know if she had done anything or not. You have to risk the wrong answer to find the right answer. Unless you are ready to exist with no answer, just drift in a blind embryo of dead, passionless safety.

I dressed, slipped my old pistol into my pocket again, and went out for some breakfast. I had eggs, over light, and looked up the name of the "friend" Francesca Crawford had sent letters to with notes in them for Felicia. Muriel Roark was the name, and her address was listed. When I went out to my car, a cold October drizzle had started.

The address was in the University section of Dresden, an old area torn down and rebuilt into low apartments and residence halls. Muriel Roark lived on the second floor of a garden apartment where the shrubbery was already sodden with rain.

A dazzling brunette opened the apartment door. Small and round, with a bright face that made me want to sing for youth, and feel old at the same time.

"Yes?"

"Miss Roark?"

She nodded, smiled. "Have we met? I like your face."

"Dan Fortune," I said, smiled back. "I want to talk about Francesca and Felicia Crawford."

Her face became serious. "Come in."

She ushered me to a long couch in a small living room. The couch was covered by a throw rug in the European style. All the furniture was old, covered with throws, and marked as her own. She flopped on a great, shapeless sack in the center of the room, showing smooth, hard thighs that had muscles. She saw my eyes looking at her legs.

"I'm a dancer," she said, raising her leg out stiff so I could see the muscles cord. "I teach modern dance at the University, a graduate fellow. What about Francesca?"

"You were good friends?"

"We understood each other. She was a private person, so am I. With her it was her scar, her identity. With me it's my dancing—no one touches that, not ever."

"You can't be touched?" I said. I liked this girl—woman.

She laughed. A warm laugh. "All I'm careful about is my muscles. You're looking for who killed Fran?"

"And for where Felicia is," I said. "You had some letters from Francesca? You showed them to Felicia?"

"No, I didn't show her my letters. I gave her two notes enclosed for her. I didn't read her notes, either."

"Damn," I said. "You can't tell me anything about what was in those notes to Felicia?"

She pulled her knees up to her chin. There was something pure and innocent about her body and its free actions.

"No," she said, "except that the first one was from somewhere out west. The letter I got was mailed from Chicago, but Felicia said the note had been written in Arizona, or Colorado, or somewhere like that."

I remembered the Indian jewelry. "You can't say which?"

"No, I'm sorry. The second letter was from New York just after Fran moved in with Celia Bazer."

"She wrote she was with Celia Bazer?" I said, sat up. "Did anyone else know that up here?"

"Only Frank Keefer. He'd come around a few times after Fran left to ask if I'd heard from her. I guess he was pretty unhappy about losing her. Anyway, about two weeks ago was the first time I could tell him anything, so I did."

"That Francesca was living with Celia Bazer?"

"Yes."

"Where does Keefer live?"

She told me. I stood up. She watched me, and seemed to stretch. Not a dancer showing her muscles this time. She stretched her whole slim, curved body.

"You have to leave?"

"Yes."

"How did you lose your arm?"

"I usually say in the war," I said. "But I really lost it in a fall into the hold of a freighter I was robbing when I was sixteen. I got away, but I lost the arm."

"Will you come back again?" she said. "Come back. Call me first. In the evening."

I could still see her lying there on that shapeless sack as I went down the stairs.

Frank Keefer's house was in a middle-class tract on the eastern edge of Dresden. There were flower beds around the small house as if someone spent a lot of time in the garden. I didn't think it was Keefer, but you never can tell—axe murderers have grown prize roses. The garage was empty, but I saw movement in the house.

Celia Bazer answered my ring. She had a discolored left eye, and her face was puffy. In the last few days she had changed from big city career girl to a small city woman, not even as pretty suddenly. She wore an old house dress, and her eyes were vacant as if she had been thinking of something important when I surprised her.

"You?" she said, groped for my name. "Mr. Fortune?"

"Yes. Can I come in?"

"Here?" she said. Her voice was vague, distracted, almost drugged. "I mean, have you found who killed Fran?"

"I'm still looking," I said.

An alarm must have sounded in her head. "How did you find me here?"

"I didn't. I want Frank Keefer. Is he home, Celia?"

"Frank?" Now her eyes were wary. "No. Why do you want Frank?"

"I'll tell you inside," I said, and gently walked her backward into a small living room. She didn't resist.

There were chairs and sofas in the living room, but everything was hidden under piles of paper, and a mimeograph machine stood on a table. The room was shabby, but not from poverty as much as from neglect. I saw a littered kitchen through an open archway, stacked with the same mimeographed pages.

I said, "I know about you, and Frank, and Francesca. Where is Frank?"

"I don't know. He never came back last night. After he did this," she touched her battered eye, "he went out with Joel."

Her voice was a monotone, as vacant as her eyes. "A year I was away, and he whistled, and here I am. He's a bastard, and a fake, but he turns me on. It's that simple, I guess, even with black eyes. Some women have no brains. I don't know, I feel . . . safe with Frank, you know? Without Joel maybe . . ."

She trailed off, her voice almost wistful, like some beaten-down wife who dreamed of her man being better some day, sure that underneath he was a good man or why would she want him?

"You know where they were all night?"

"No. Part of their new scheme, I guess." She nodded toward all the piles of literature. "Joel talked a couple of local shopping centers into a throwaway newsletter, said he could get it into the northwest suburbs, the rich people. He told them he could get a special deal because he's with the city, everything cut-rate. All the merchants in the centers take ads, and Frank runs the things off on the mimeo. I hope they make the price of the ink."

"You don't distribute leaflets at night," I said.

"Maybe they got into a poker game, or another deal."

"Do either of them know Abram Zaremba?"

"Commissioner Zaremba? You mean personally? Maybe if they shined his shoes once."

"They know anything about the Black Mountain Lake project?"

She nodded. "Joel got the Mayor to appoint him an inspector of the drainage district out there, and he got Frank in to sell lots. Only it was hard to sell them so early, Frank didn't like the job." She stopped, surprised. "What's that got to do with Francesca?"

"Maybe a lot, Celia," I said. "Frank lied about not knowing Francesca was with you in New York."

"Lied?" Some life came into her voice as she realized the only way I could have known Frank Keefer had denied knowing that Francesca was in New York with her. "You were at that hotel. You followed me there. What makes you say Frank lied?"

I told her what Murial Roark had told me. "Frank admits he was in New York when Francesca was killed."

"But he never saw her."

"Didn't he? He was asking about her since she left. He's not a man who gives up, is he? He went there to see her, Celia. After she was dead he turned to you, maybe to cover up."

"No, he loves me. All right he lives big dreams, so if he could marry Francesca, swell, but she dropped him." Her monotone was flat again. "Anyway, he wouldn't kill her."

"Unless maybe he made a mistake, Celia?" I said. "You said that in the hotel. A bad mistake, you said."

"I don't know what you mean," she said.

"Yes, you do," I said. "Francesca died in your bed.

She had slept in your bed that night. A mistake, maybe, made by someone who wanted to kill you not her?"

She had thought about it. "My bed was better, that's all."

"Frank Keefer wouldn't have known that. What could you have told Francesca that would have finished Frank with her for good if it wasn't over already?"

She shook her head.

"I'll find out somehow, Celia. I have the police on my side, they'll check out his life with a microscope. If he tried to kill you, got the wrong girl, you've got to know one way or the other, don't you?"

She shook her head again. Wildly, like a rag doll, but it had no meaning now. Her monotone cracked.

"He was in prison once for wife-beating," she said, her voice so low I could barely hear it. "In Pennsylvania. He's still got a wife there. A boy, too. He sends money sometimes. I don't care. I didn't like New York, I didn't like the men there. I just want Frank."

"He's married, but he'd have married Francesca?"

"Why not? Who would know? His name was Pender then, like Joel's. He lives lies, even believes them himself. It isn't what a man is, it's what he thinks he is—Joel says that. It isn't who you are, it's who people think you are. Joel's got a million sayings."

"If Keefer tried to get Francesca back, went down there to make a play, would that have made you tell Francesca what you knew? Would he have tried to stop you telling if he thought he had a chance with Francesca?"

She was silent. Then, "I always wanted Frank, even when he threw me over and I went to New York. He knew that. I might have told. But Frank's no killer, it's not in him."

"A man who lives by lies, believes his own lies?"

She didn't answer. I wanted her to think about it.

I said, "Who's Joel Pender, Celia?"

"Frank's uncle. From out west somewhere, always talking about cowboys. He's been all over, I guess, a drifter. Frank always looked up to Joel, the exciting uncle when Frank was a kid in Pennsylvania. To me Joel's a bum, but he's mean and tough for his size. Half Frank's size, and Frank's afraid of him. When he's drunk he boasts about being some kind of bodyguard once, running gambling games. I've seen him carry a gun sometimes even now."

"Why does the Mayor give him jobs? Patronage?"

"Who knows? The Mayor likes him, I guess. He worked for the Mayor once a long time ago. Worked for that old man Emil Van Hoek, too. The Mayor's wife's father, you know?"

"Celia," I said, "if Frank killed Francesca, and someone knew that, Frank would kill again, wouldn't he?"

"Frank wouldn't kill any—"

They were there in the living room. Two of them. One was Frank Keefer. The other was a scrawny little man with a dark, weather-beaten face, his small eyes sunk in deep sockets. He wore a cheap suit, looked sixty but I knew was younger, and stood tall for his five-feet-six or so. He moved more like his real age—maybe forty-five despite the aged face. He came low and fast toward my armless side, while Frank Keefer charged straight at me.

I tried to duck, and took a roundhouse right lead on my head that knocked me over a chair. The chair got in Keefer's way, and I got up and jumped to the right away from the small man. I dug into my pocket for my pistol.

"Keefer, hold it!" I cried. "I just want—"

Keefer wasn't listening. He charged like a bull, and I evaded again, staying away from the little man. Celia Bazer was screaming at Keefer. The small man grabbed her, slapped her face, and Keefer came on again, his big fists ready. I had no choice. I slipped aside again—he was an awkward amateur—and hit him across the face with my pistol.

He howled, a long line of red blood on his cheek, but tried once more. I hit him on the mouth with the gun. Blood spurted at me. He grabbed for his broken mouth, sat down on the floor, and stared up at me in disbelief.

I waved the gun at the scrawny one. "Get over near him."

The small man went. In the corner Celia Bazer nursed her slapped face. The two men glared at me, Keefer moaning.

CHAPTER FOURTEEN

"You're a rough pair, you are," I said. "Why?"

"You always go around accusing people of murder?" the scrawny one said.

Now I saw that his cheap suit had been retailored to look handmade, his shirt was dazzlingly white, and something glittered in his tie. A stickpin, with a chip diamond set to look twice its size.

"You said I killed Fran!" Frank Keefer mumbled through blood and broken teeth. He stared at a tooth in his hand, incredulous and afraid of any injury.

"Did you?" I said.

"Why should he, mister?" the small one said. "That kid was our trip to heaven. If you're here, you know that."

He had drifter and con man written all over him. His cheap clothes made to look flashy with fake touches a drifter learns in a hundred vagrant tanks. I guessed that there had been times when he'd had newspaper for a shirt and burlap for shoes. The kind of sharp, clever face that always lost out no matter how much he schemed, because he was never quite smart enough to carry a scheme through. But there was violence, too. Violence of the kind that is dangerous when it has a bigger power behind it—bodyguard, vigilante, deputy sheriff.

"You're Joel Pender?" I said.

He didn't like my knowing his name. It was pure habit—a man who automatically tried to hide himself.

"I don't know you, mister," he said.

"Dan Fortune. I'm a private detective looking for

Francesca Crawford's killer. The New York police are in my corner. All I have to do is whistle."

"Then whistle and damn you!" Frank Keefer said through his broken mouth. "Look at my face!"

"It'll heal and give you character," I said. "Why start fights when you can't fight? Maybe you just thought it would be easy to beat a one-armed man? Fight cripples?"

"You were pumping Celia, cripple," Joel Pender said. He was a sweet man. "Why don't you talk to us straight?"

"Fine," I said. "Keefer, what did you talk about down in New York with Francesca Crawford? When you visited her?"

"I never went down to Fran—"

Celia Bazer spoke from her corner. "He was in that hotel, Frank. He heard us talking."

"Heard?" Frank Keefer said, licked blood.

"Heard," I said. "All of it, including lies. Muriel Roark told you Francesca was with Celia, and you got down to New York on Tuesday—the day she was killed."

"I never went near her!"

"You didn't know she was alone in the apartment?"

"No! I didn't know Cele wasn't back until after—"

Joel Pender said, "Shut up, Frank. This guy's got something in mind."

I said, "You thought Celia might be back, would be in her own bed that Tuesday night?"

"I didn't go near the place until Wednesday," Keefer said.

"No," I said. "You were seen Tuesday evening. Maybe you came back that night, climbed in the window looking for Celia who would tell Francesca you still had a wife, had served time for wife-beating. You had made a new play for Francesca, maybe she gave you some hope. But if Celia knew, and talked . . . ? So you came to kill Celia. It was dark, you were scared, Celia's bed was occupied. Who else would be in that bed? So you stabbed her—only Celia wasn't back, and you killed Francesca."

Frank Keefer forgot his bleeding mouth. Only abject fear would make him do that. A fear that saw himself facing a judge, convicted, waiting to be sentenced to some narrow cell for the rest of his natural life—no more schemes, no more women, no more dreams of a golden future.

"You're a liar!" he said.

Joel Pender faced danger a different way—with a sharp, cool calculation. His teeth ready, careful.

"He's fishing, Frank," Pender said. "If it happened like he says, no one could prove it, and he wouldn't be talking."

"Unless Frank was seen that night," I said.

"I couldn't have been," Keefer said. "I wasn't there. Anyway, I couldn't have—"

"Shut up, Frank," Pender said, and to me, "Who saw Frank?"

"Maybe Abram Zaremba, or one of his men checking up on Francesca," I said. "He was killed last night, and where were you two last night?"

"Commissioner Zaremba?" Frank Keefer said, shaky.

Joel Pender had nothing to say.

I said, "It looks like Zaremba could have known who murdered Francesca. She saw the killer of Mark Leland, who was investigating the Black Mountain Lake project. Maybe Zaremba was having her tailed, at least, just to be sure she knew nothing vital. She was down in New York for a reason, I'm sure—hiding, using a false name, meeting older men. For all I know she could have been mixed with you two in some scheme to stop Zaremba, a little blackmail, or—"

Frank Keefer said, turning to Joel Pender, "Tell him, Joel! Tell him what Fran was doing. I don't want to be tied in with any murder of Commissioner Zaremba, no way!"

"I told you to shut up," Pender said.

His voice was quiet, but his eyes were busy. He was balancing the risk against the gain—the calculation and infinite patience of a small weasel who would crawl ten years on his belly if he had a reasonable assurance that at the end he would make others crawl.

"I'll tell you what we figure the kid was doing in New York," he said, "if you keep quiet about who told you first. Okay, Fortune? I'll deny it anyway."

"Tell me," I said.

Frank Keefer mopped his bloody mouth like a woman seeing the first gray hair. Celia Bazer still stood in her corner as if she felt safer with two walls close. Pender leaned toward me, sincere. I guessed it was an act he'd practiced.

"I was drunk or it'd never happened," Pender said. "She came here that night all shook up. Said she'd found out her dad was a fraud, cheating the public to help men like Commissioner Zaremba and get rich himself. She said she knew I knew about the Mayor, and she wanted me to tell her. Some legal trick in the Mayor's past Leland had told her about. She didn't know what it was because Leland hadn't known. I said I didn't know anything, and Frank tried to calm her down. So then she turned on Frank and said she was through with him!

"She said we were all liars and cheats, too, and Frank was a lousy gigolo. We were worse than her dad or Zaremba because we worked for them like parasites, did their dirty work. She was in one hell of a state, and when she told Frank they was finished, I got so mad I lost my head. Our big chance, see? Marry into the Mayor's family, be someone in this town. Gone for a lousy girl kid thought she was too good for us, too good even for the Mayor! So damned holy about the Mayor being a cheat and all. I just saw red, damn her!"

He shook his head, and his small eyes were mystified, as if he would never understand how a smart man like himself had been so stupid, had been goaded into saying what he had not wanted to say. He shrugged up at me.

"So I told her," he said. "I told her she lived on the Mayor, went to college on the Mayor, learned all her big, pure ideas on the Mayor. So he got something for himself out of his job, why not? If he was a fraud and a cheat, she lived on him, and there were men a lot worse than the Mayor. I told her she should get down on her knees to the Mayor for giving her all she had because he didn't have to give her spit!"

Pender stopped again. He was having a hard time telling it even now. I didn't push him. He sighed.

"I was drunk, see, so I told her what no one ever told her before. I said if she thought the Mayor was a crook, maybe she ought to know there was a lot worse crooks like murderers, kidnappers, and psychos—and she was the kid of one of those! She was the kid of a guy who shot her grandfather, got her shot, and damned near got her mother killed, too!"

He looked at me. "I told her Crawford wasn't her real father. Not hers, and not Felicia's. Her old lady was married before, a long time ago, and her real father almost got them all killed, and went to prison for twenty years for it!"

In the silence of that room piled with the mimeographed dream of a quick profit for two losers, I suppose we all had our own thoughts. Pender chewed his lip, probably still wondering why he'd blurted it all out to Francesca in drunken anger over three months ago. A secret that explained why Pender got jobs from Mayor Crawford. Keefer was probably thinking only of himself, of the loss of his hopes for marrying big. Celia Bazer seemed to be wondering how she'd feel at such news.

I was seeing pieces of a puzzle fall into place like greased parts of a complex machine. Francesca's excitement. Her oblique talk about identity—it had been real, not just metaphorical: her real identity at stake. Her sudden trip—a girl who'd always felt different, neglected, a rebel, the ugly duckling. Looking for a real father. What all the men in New York she'd met had in common was clear—they were all over forty. Except Abram Zaremba, who was older, but she hadn't really met him, only gone to work at his restaurant in a job she didn't need. So the Emerald Room was, somehow, connected to her father. It explained everything, except why she had been using a false name, and maybe Mark Leland's murder still explained that. Maybe she wanted to find a lost father for more than her identity—for help in trouble, too.

"Tell me the whole story, Pender," I said. "What else did you tell Francesca?"

"That's all," Pender said. "Her old lady was married young, busted up, married Crawford, and then the first guy came around and started a shooting match and went to jail for it. Happened before I was around here, I only got it secondhand. Only I was here three years later when the first husband busted prison and got killed in the escape."

"Francesca's real father is dead?" I said.

"Like a dinosaur," Joel Pender said, and laughed. "Those girl twins was lucky. Crawford brought 'em up like white women, when their real old man was a crummy Indian from some two-bit reservation out west."

"An Indian?"

"That's how I heard it. Man, that must of sat big around here. No wonder Katje Crawford dumped him."

"How did Francesca take it?"

"Like I'd slapped her. Said I was a liar at first. I told her go ask old Emil Van Hoek if her folks wouldn't tell her, and I figured they wouldn't. Bad blood, that was what she had, and she was going around calling the Mayor a fraud when he'd brought her up like his real own kids."

"You think Francesca went looking for her real father," I said, "even though he was dead?"

"Sure she did. Maybe she didn't believe me, wanted proof."

Celia Bazer said, her voice low from the corner, "Maybe she wanted to know about him, her real father, know who he was. Maybe she just wanted to know what really happened."

She said it as if she, if she had been Francesca, would have wanted to know who her father had been, what had really happened a long time ago.

"All right," I said. "Don't go anywhere. I don't think Mayor Crawford'll thank you for telling her."

Frank Keefer said nothing, went on gingerly touching his broken face which was all that interested him. Pender glared an inner anger at himself for being so stupid, for getting drunk and losing his temper. Celia Bazer stood silent in her corner, maybe hoping no one would think of her after I was gone, not until it was time to go to bed.

CHAPTER FIFTEEN

I drove thinking about a girl who went looking for a dead father. Yes, Francesca would have done that. A man might die, but he left a shadow, a life, a place of his own, relatives, all the things a girl who felt rejected and different would want to know. Death ends only a man, not the life he had lived, the place where he had belonged. Above all the place—somewhere in this world where, maybe, his daughter could belong, too, as she had never belonged among the Crawfords, and Van Hoeks, and Black Mountain Lake projects for the benefit of Abram Zarembas.

Would that search have killed her? It depended on what she turned over in the search, on a lot of things I didn't know. Did Felicia know? I thought Felicia did— part of it anyway. Not as much, maybe, but enough to make her want to know who had hired me and what I knew. Enough to send her on the same search herself?

I stopped to call Lieutenant Oster. He had news.

"They picked up your client, John Andera, down in New York," Oster said. "He was on a selling trip in Philadelphia. It checks out solid with witnesses down there. His alibi is good for the Crawford girl, too— another business trip."

"What about Mrs. Grace Dunstan?"

"Not so good for her. She was in New Haven, but no one saw her from eight P.M. last night until past one A.M. She could have driven to Dresden. Harmon Dunstan isn't covered for the time of Zaremba's death, either."

I told him what Joel Pender had told me. "Is it true?"

101

"As far as I know. Before my time," Oster said, and there was a pause. "Mayor Crawford isn't going to like Pender. It's old dirty linen. Dead and buried."

"Maybe not so buried," I said. "Where do I talk to the grandmother? Old Mrs. Van Hoek?"

"She's got a cottage on the Mayor's place. What do you think she can tell you?"

"I'll know when I ask her."

"Take it easy, Fortune."

"I always do, Lieutenant," I said, and hung up.

I drove on to the Crawford mansion, parked up the road. The small cottage was in the rear among the trees, the rain dripping onto its roof. I knocked. The woman who opened the door after a time was tall, thin, white-haired, and dressed in a formal black dress without any decoration. The white hair was in a severe bun, and her long, thin face was severe too.

"Yes?" she said, and added, "You're that detective."

"Dan Fortune, Mrs. Van Hoek. Can we talk?"

"About what?"

The question wasn't challenging, only neutral, implying that she had nothing to talk about. I saw that her severe manner was more disassociated than stern. The manner of someone who lived alone with her own slow thoughts.

"About Francesca and your husband," I said.

"I never knew anything about Francesca. Mr. Van Hoek is dead," she said, and turned away as if that settled it all.

I followed her into a small Victorian room that had an aura of timeless insulation. She sat down, as timeless as the room, and neither looked at me nor away from me. She didn't seem surprised that I had not closed the door behind me and gone away, but her eyes seemed uninterested by me. I had an impression that we were both in the same room, but in different times, therefore invisible to each other.

"Your husband died suddenly." I said.

She looked toward a window and the rain. "Mr. Van Hoek took many years to die."

"He talked with Francesca just before he died," I said.

The rain on the windows seemed to fascinate her. "I liked the rain as a girl. It was so warm in the attic of the big house where we played. That was before I met Mr. Van Hoek. Katje and the Mayor have the big house now. It's not the same house, that was torn down years ago. I live here. As long as I live I have a home here. Katje is a good daughter."

"Did Mr. Van Hoek tell Francesca about Katje's first husband, Mrs. Van Hoek?"

"I don't know. Leave me alone, please."

She sat in her chair as if she didn't want to move, not ever, for fear of breaking time into small pieces, of losing her own image in the shattered mirror of time.

"Katje's first husband was an Indian?"

"A nice boy. She brought him home twice. She was defiant, you see? He was a soldier, away from home. She had it annulled. The best way. The Mayor was better for the children."

"You opposed the marriage? The Indian boy?"

"There were the children. He was a nice boy, but we couldn't make her try. She knew what she wanted to do."

"You wanted her to make the marriage work?"

"She knew better. You can see that. We have a fine home."

"But he came back, the Indian. Made trouble?"

She moved her head in a sharp jerk. "Leave me alone, please. I don't want to talk to you."

I heard steps coming toward the cottage. At the window, I looked out and saw a small man with silver-gray hair coming toward the cottage under an umbrella. He walked stiffly, like a judge—or a senior lawyer. How did I know? I don't know, but it was an impression, and his face was too young for his silver-gray hair and his manner. Prematurely gray.

I went back to Mrs. Van Hoek as the gray-haired man came into the cottage. He shook his umbrella outside, laid it just inside the door, turned, and came into the living room smiling and rubbing his hands against the October cold. He saw me.

"Who are you?"

"Dan Fortune, Mr.—?"

"Carter Vance. You're the private detective? What the hell are you doing with Mrs. Van Hoek?"

His diction didn't quite match his silver hair or his formal clothes. Neither did his age—about forty or so. As if he'd built a careful public image to hide himself.

"I'm talking with Mrs. Van Hoek," I said.

The old woman said, "I don't want to talk to him."

"You heard her," Carter Vance said.

"Vance?" I said. "Mayor Crawford's law partner, right? Head of the Crime Commission with Anthony Sasser. I'll bet you turned up a lot about Abram Zaremba's dealings."

"I don't understand, Mr. Fortune," Vance said.

"Sasser worked with Zaremba, right?"

"If you're implying that Mr. Zaremba did anything illegal, be careful. We found no such situation. We did manage to clean up the streets of Dresden, though."

"I'll bet you really cracked down on pickpockets and welfare cheats. Two-bit hoodlums stay clear of Dresden, right? Honest citizens can make an honest dollar in peace and safety so they can pay their taxes for Abram Zaremba's benefit."

"Not all two-bit hoodlums stay clear of Dresden, it seems," Vance said. "Mrs. Van Hoek doesn't want to talk to you."

"I want to talk to her," I said, and turned back to her. "If you could just tell me what your husband told Fran—"

"Fortune," Vance said.

He had a gun. A blue Mauser automatic. He waved it toward the door.

"You better ask Martin Crawford anything you want to know."

"You always carry a gun, Vance?" I said.

"I head a crime commission. I have the need. Now walk."

I walked.

We walked, dripping rain, through the entry hall of the Crawford mansion. Martin Crawford sat in the living room reading the newspaper. He lumbered up when he saw us.

"Carter? What the devil—?" he said, looked at us both.

Vance said, "He was in the cottage, annoying the old lady with questions. He didn't want to leave."

Katje Crawford appeared from somewhere. "Put down that gun, Carter. Mr. Fortune is a detective."

"A cheap snooper from New York," Vance said. "I think we can charge him with trespassing. He refused to leave."

"He just wants to help us, Carter," Martin Crawford said.

"Help?" Vance said. He pocketed his gun, walked out to the glassed-in porch, began to pour himself a drink.

Katje Crawford came all the way into the living room. She wore a tweed skirt, a cashmere sweater, low shoes, and a golf glove on her right hand as if still hoping the rain would stop.

"Why did you want to talk to my mother?" she asked.

"To find out what your father told Francesca just before she left home," I said.

"My father?"

"Told Francesca what, Fortune?" Martin Crawford asked.

Katje Crawford sat down. "I wasn't aware that my

father had seen Francesca before she left. He was very sick."

"What do you think he told her, Fortune?" Crawford said.

"Something about her real father," I said.

It didn't exactly hit them like a bombshell, no. They had lived with it for a long time. But saying it out like that startled them. They had kept it so far hidden that it must have sounded almost strange to them said out loud. Carter Vance turned at the bar, looked at me and at them.

"So you know," Martin Crawford said. "I suppose I knew you would. One tries hard to shelter a child. For Francesca it's too late, but I had hoped to keep it from Felicia a bit longer. It's not easy to be a stepfather, it changes a child's relation to you. To me they're my children, but I've always known they would see me differently if they knew the truth."

I said, "Has Felicia come home?"

"No," Crawford said.

There was a world of pain in the single word. Crawford had lost one daughter, or stepdaughter, and his voice said that he didn't want to lose another.

Katje Crawford said, "You think my father told Francesca something about her real father, and that's connected to her death somehow?"

"I don't know what he told her, or what it means."

She shook her head. "I can't think what he could have said that would have any bearing, Mr. Fortune."

"Can you tell me about it all?" I said.

Katje Crawford sat and thought for a time. Then she nodded slowly. "Very well, sit down, Mr. Fortune. I don't see what good it can do, but I expect you'll go on searching until you know the story."

I sat. Martin Crawford leaned back in his chair, his hands over his eyes, as if he didn't want to hear. Carter Vance sipped his drink out on the porch.

CHAPTER SIXTEEN

"His name was Ralph Blackwind," Katje Crawford said, and smiled thinly. "I think the name fascinated me. It was so strong, ethnic. I was seventeen in 1950, in New York alone trying to be a dancer. I had no talent. Too tall, awkward. So many young people desperately want to be what they can never be. As if they purposely choose the dream that must defeat them because they are equipped for it least of all they could do. Perhaps it's necessary to learn the pain of failure before you can turn back to what you really knew you had to be all along. The real tragedy is the few who go on pursuing a hopeless dream, just good enough for a few small triumphs, hope always just ahead."

She stopped to find a cigarette. I waited. She would tell it all in her own way. Out on the porch, Carter Vance was mixing another drink. His own was still half-full, so it wasn't for him. Crawford sat like a man watching an old movie he'd seen fifty times before and knew by heart.

"Ralph Blackwind," Katje Crawford said, smoked. "I met him at a YMCA dance for soldiers. He was handsome, dark-eyed, small and stocky, intense and all male. I was seventeen, in a hurry to be a woman. We were both outdoor people, we used to ride in New Jersey. He wanted a ranch among his people, work with them. Dedicated, coiled like a whip. I'm not a fool, I was failing as a dancer, and I knew it. I needed a new dream, Ralph was it. After a month we were married. But Korea had broken out, and two months later Ralph was sent over there, and I came home. Of course, I was pregnant by then."

She looked up at me. "I was pregnant, Ralph was in Korea, and I knew it was wrong, a mistake, an error. The moment I came home, I knew it. Ralph and I— here? With what I knew all at once I really wanted? My life here? It had been a childish dream worse than the dancing. I knew, but Ralph was fighting in Korea. Could I write and tell him? I couldn't. So the girls were born, twins. Francesca and Felicia Blackwind."

The names were exotic in the big, elegant room. They had a wild sound, open and windy in a dry land of desert hills.

"God," Martin Crawford said, "how Francesca would have liked that name. We should have told her, Katje, the moment we saw what kind of tough girl she was."

"Perhaps we should have," Katje Crawford said, and said to me, "I met Martin again soon after the twins were born. He'd known me when I was a girl. We fell in love. We were right for each other—the same lives, the same backgrounds, the same plans for the future. What were we to do? I couldn't divorce Ralph, by then he'd been reported missing in action! Martin was in politics, it would have been suicide to try a divorce. We waited and waited, but Ralph wasn't found, and the girls were growing. So we had the marriage quietly annulled, and were married ourselves. A year later, Ralph came home."

She stubbed out her cigarette. It was almost a vicious gesture. Carter Vance brought her the drink he had made. She took it and drank without looking at Vance.

"Ralph had been a prisoner of the North Koreans for almost two years. He'd escaped—alone across hundreds of miles of enemy territory. He'd killed many of the enemy, some with his hands. Something had changed in him. He was cold, bitter, a man who could kill easily. Perhaps that had always been part of him, in his history, in his anger at being an Indian.

"He learned of the birth of the girls, and of our annulment. I suppose something snapped when they told him. A combination of what he'd been through, of the shock of the news. Perhaps it was only a last straw. He talked about death, the horror of war, the horror of the whole world, the insanity of the white man's world. He wanted his haven—me and his children."

She recrossed her legs. "I don't pretend to think that I acted well to Ralph. I never wrote to him about the girls, I had the marriage annulled without telling him. Yes, I thought he was dead over there, perhaps I even hoped he was, but that was no excuse. I did what I had to do for my own life. We had made a mistake, Ralph and I, and Ralph would have known that, too, if we had tried to go on. I had to correct it. Firm and final. There was no other way."

She drank the drink Carter Vance had given to her, and seemed to realize she had it for the first time. She stared into the drink. "I was living with my parents while Martin was in Albany. That weekend, Martin was on his way home, but he hadn't arrived yet. I've always given thanks for that. I think Ralph would have killed Martin.

"He walked into the house with a submachine gun and a pistol. All I did was move, and he started shooting. He shattered the living room, and hit my father! He almost killed my father. He made me get the children, and drove away with us. We drove all evening toward Canada. The girls had to eat and sleep, so he stopped in a motel in Utica. That was when I learned all about Korea, his escape, his anger at the world. He talked to me all night while the children slept as much as they could, they were so afraid.

"He talked and talked that night, about all his horrors, and about his plans for a ranch in Canada. Nonstop, as if he really were insane.

"I've seen that night in my dreams a thousand times since, and I'm still sorry for Ralph, terribly sorry for what he had become in that war, for what I had had to do. But I have never regretted it. The girls had nightmares for years afterwards. He would have been hounded down eventually, and who knows what would have happened to the girls? I did what was right."

She stopped, and sat back in her chair. She lighted another cigarette. She smoked as if that was all, the story over as far as she was concerned—she had done right.

"How did you get away from him?" I asked.

"The police came in the morning," she said, her voice normal now. "Martin had arrived home soon after Ralph took us. He saved my father, and alerted the police. When they found us, Ralph tried to resist, and Francesca was shot in the melee. That was her scar, Mr. Fortune. Under it all, Ralph wasn't a bad man. When Francesca was hit, he gave up, carried her out to an ambulance himself."

I said, "Then?"

Martin Crawford said, "I defended Blackwind. I had Katje say she had gone with him voluntarily, to talk to him, and I had the kidnapping charge dropped. I got it all dropped—except the assault-with-intent-to-murder on Katje's father. Mr. Van Hoek had been badly shot, and we couldn't evade that charge even though he pulled through. Blackwind got ten-to-twenty in Auburn. Three years later he escaped with four other men. One was killed in the escape—so was a prison guard. Ralph and the other two evaded capture for three days. Two of them were cornered in Hancock, one was killed. The survivor said that Ralph had drowned in a Catskill lake where they'd hidden."

"They found his body?"

"Not at first. They found his weapons at the lake, the food he'd been carrying, but nothing else. So they continued the manhunt for five months. They ran down every lead, every report, everyone who had known Ralph. No trace of him was found, not a whisper that he was alive anywhere. Then divers found a body in the lake, wedged under rocks. It was bloated and eaten beyond any recognition, but it was Ralph's size, had the remnants of his clothes, and his identification. It had been in the water the exact time. He'd dead, Mr. Fortune."

For a time we were all silent. I knew what we were all thinking—was Ralph Blackwind alive somewhere? Perhaps somewhere not very far?

Carter Vance broke the spell. "I never knew the whole story. He was already dead when I came to town. Awful."

Katje Crawford said, "You think that Ralph is alive, Mr. Fortune?"

"Any time a body isn't positively identified, you have to consider that, yes," I said. "What about dental records, scars, wounds, old injuries?"

Crawford said, "Blackwind had no dental work beyond his childhood, and his reservation had no records. The body was too decomposed to show scars. His brother said he had broken his left arm once, and there was a break in the left arm of the body. Only it was a recent break, and the M.E. couldn't say if it was a new break or the old one rebroken. The reservation had no X-ray records."

"But the left arm did have the break?"

Katje Crawford said, "He's dead, Mr. Fortune. How could he have eluded such a manhunt so completely, and how could there have been a body his size in that lake just at the right time? If he was alive, he would have tried to see the girls sometime during the last fifteen years. He had a tremendous love of children, I hadn't known that about him. In fact, I knew so little about him."

"Would Francesca search for a dead man?" I said.

"Perhaps, yes. For her identity, for the truth about her history. She'd want to know about Ralph."

Crawford said, "And she wouldn't ask us, no."

"Was Abram Zaremba connected to Blackwind at all?"

"Not at all, as far as I know," Crawford said.

"How about a Carl Gans? John Andera? Harmon Dunstan? Or maybe Joel Pender, or Frank Keefer, or Anthony Sasser?"

"No, none of them," Katje Crawford said. "Tony Sasser wasn't even in Dresden before Ralph was dead."

Crawford said, "Wait. There was a Captain Dunstan at Ralph's trial, Katje. His commanding officer in Korea, captured with Ralph, remember? He testified for Ralph."

"I don't remember, Martin," Katje Crawford said. "It's been fifteen years now."

"Are you sure, Crawford?" I said.

"Pretty sure, yes. Captain Dunstan."

"All right, maybe Francesca went searching out her past and a dead father. Maybe it has something to do with why she was killed, and maybe not. It could be a coincidence, or she could have stumbled over something dangerous, or someone could even have made a mistake about what she was after," I said to them. "But maybe we better remember one thing—if Ralph Blackwind does happen to be still alive, he's got the murder of a prison guard hanging over him still. He might do a lot to not be found."

None of them had an answer for that. Katje Crawford sat looking at the floor when I left. Maybe she was wondering if none of this would have happened if she had told the girls about their father a long time ago.

In my car, I drove back to my motel and checked out. As I drove south and east through the rain, it all came into focus. Francesca had been looking for her father. Now Felicia was. Dead or alive, I didn't know. Maybe that was what the grandfather, Emil Van Hoek, had had to tell Francesca—one way or the other.

CHAPTER SEVENTEEN

I stopped for lunch on the road, and it was late afternoon when I crossed the Throggs Neck Bridge and drove across the Island to Hempstead. The rain had stopped, the day clear and bright with a touch of early winter in its snap.

There were two cars in Harmon Dunstan's garage. No one seemed to be watching this time, but when I rang at the door, not much else had changed. Mrs. Grace Dunstan opened the door in almost the same shirt and slacks, and with the same Bloody Mary in her hand. I had the sensation of time standing still. She looked at me as if time did stand still for her—one day exactly like another, the same things in the same way with no surprises and no need to think about tomorrow because it would be today and yesterday over again. A weariness in her.

"Mr. Fortune," she said like fate. "Come in then."

Harmon Dunstan sat at the home bar in the immaculate living room, a drink in his slender hand this time. It was late enough now, maybe in more ways than one. Dunstan was less friendly this time, his thin, dark face slack and watchful.

"You sent the police last night?" the small man said.

"The Dresden police sent them. Your wife was in New Haven—just about unseen. Where were you?"

"Calling on a client in Westchester," Dunstan said. "My bad luck, he wasn't at home—called away suddenly."

"Did you know Abram Zaremba?"

"No. I don't like people coming here with threats."

113

"I haven't made any threats."

"You—" He ended it there. The threat was in his mind, and he was smart enough to realize he had revealed that.

I said, "What did Francesca Crawford really want from you, Dunstan?"

"I've told you all I'm going to, Fortune."

Grace Dunstan said, "Talk to him, Harmon. Your women are no real secret. Everyone knows we have an understanding."

"Be quiet, Grace," Dunstan said. It was firm, but gentle. Telling her that she didn't know what she was saying.

I said, "What did she want, Dunstan? She made a play for you, yet she lost interest fast. Did she think you could help her to find out about her father?"

"Her father?" Dunstan said.

It wasn't a question, no, not even rhetorical. It was footwork, something to say while he thought. He finished his drink, keeping busy to keep from talking. Grace Dunstan took his glass, and began to refill it. She worked with one hand, drinking her own Bloody Mary while she made his drink.

"Ralph Blackwind," I said. "You remember him? You were his captain in Korea. You testified for him at his trial."

"Yes," Dunstan said, "I remember him."

"Did Francesca ask about him?"

"Yes, she asked about him," Dunstan said. His wife gave him his new drink. He drank. "I told her that Ralph had died fifteen years ago. That he got a raw deal, went to prison, and died. I told her that he was a good man who had deserved better, but that's the way the ball bounces. She had her mother and a good life, let Ralph Blackwind rest in peace."

"That's all?"

"That was all."

"But it means you knew who she was before she was killed. You knew she was Francesca Crawford, not Martin."

"Yes, all right, I knew. After she asked about Ralph, I knew. What does it mean? That was all a long time ago. She was a woman here and now, I liked her, wanted her. Ralph was old history. It was the present I was after."

"So am I," I said.

Dunstan said nothing.

"Poor Harmon," Grace Dunstan said. "You didn't get what you wanted this time, did you? This one got away."

Dunstan turned on her. "I liked her, Grace. This was real. You sensed that, didn't you? You've never cared about the women I chased before. You're not interested in me, so the other women didn't matter, and for that I thanked you. I need a woman, you don't need a man, at least not me. So you didn't care about my substitutes. They weren't good, but they were better than nothing if I couldn't have you. But this time you knew it was different."

"Did I?" she said. "Maybe you're right, but she's dead, and that ends it, doesn't it? You'll have to settle for what we have until next time. I'm sorry, really I am."

"Sorry enough to come to my bedroom sometimes?"

She turned away sharply.

I said, "You have separate bedrooms? Then your alibis for Francesca's murder are zero. It's a big house, with separate bedrooms. Either of you could come or go without being seen or heard. You can't prove where you were when Francesca was killed. No more than you can prove where you were last night."

Dunstan was silent. "Can most people prove where they were when you ask them about any given night?"

"It depends."

"On what, Fortune?"

"Mostly on luck. The chance they were with some-one."

"Then we weren't lucky," Dunstan said.

Grace Dunstan said, "We never have been, have we, Harmon?"

I had the feeling of a man standing high on a cliff looking down at two people walking a solitary beach. No one else was anywhere, yet they walked apart. Each alone in the sea and sky, unable to move together no matter how much they wanted to, or even had to because there was no one else. They walked along side-by-side, but each alone. Each staring at the horizon for someone else to come along, any new face to talk to, to smile with. Yet no one would come, because, for them, there really was no one else. Neither anyone else, nor each other, so doomed to a kind of slow dance together that would end only when one or both were dead. Two people wanting each other, without mercy on each other, and needing each other maybe more than they even knew.

I said, "You're sure Ralph Blackwind is dead, Dunstan?"

"Yes," he said, "I'm sure. I know he's dead, and now I have to leave. No more questions, Fortune, unless you come with the police and more than suspicions you can't prove."

Grace Dunstan drank and watched him go. She put down her glass, smiled at me. It was a stiff smile.

"He was rebuffed by Francesca Crawford, whether he wants to say so or not. I can tell. He's right, too, I did take more notice of her than I had of his other women. She wasn't like the women he usually toyed with. A strange girl, not his type at all. I met her twice, and I didn't think she cared about Harmon for himself at all. I didn't know about her father. She puzzled me."

"Puzzled you," I said, "and worried you?"

She considered the question and me. "Yes, she worried me. The unknown worries me. I live with the familiar, the sure. This house, our money, my furniture. Harmon and I are tied like stones on a short chain, but we're tied closely. Only I didn't kill her, Mr. Fortune."

"I hope not," I said.

I went out to my car.

CHAPTER EIGHTEEN

I had to park in a garage six blocks from the Emerald Room. I looked for a taxi, but it was five-thirty now, and I walked three blocks looking and waving. After the three blocks, I gave up, and walked to the restaurant. It had just opened.

The elegant entry greeted me with a cosy warmth that made me want to settle down at the bar for a long stay. Carl Gans didn't greet me. A bigger man seemed to have his job now. The bigger man saw my duffel coat and missing arm.

"You want something?" he said.

"I'm looking for Carl Gans."

"He's off tonight."

"Commissioner Zaremba's murder?"

"You know, huh?" He had new respect for me. I was in the know, no matter how I looked. "Yeh, Carl took it hard. He'd been like twenty years with the Commissioner. Took a week off."

"He went away?"

"Just in his pad, boozing I guess. Don't blame him, he done good with the Commissioner around."

"You have the address? It's important, about the Commissioner."

"Five-eighty West Ninety-fourth. That's at Riverside."

It was a long drive, but it would take longer to get a taxi at this hour. I went back to the garage, ransomed my car, and drove up in the night past the Park that was bare and still in the prewinter cold, the people hurrying

as the temperature dropped unseasonably and caught
them.

The building at Ninety-fourth and Riverside Drive
was an old graystone apartment from the last century. It
was not where I would have expected Carl Gans to live.
There was a reserved, muted class to the building, and
its lobby was as clean as a Dutch housewife's doorstep.
Gans had apartment 4-D. I rode up in a lumbering old
elevator, and wondered even more about Gans living
in such a quiet building. Somewhere inside the bouncer
was a man who wanted a solid, quiet life among suc-
cessful, educated people. Because a man has only muscles to earn a living, it doesn't mean that somewhere
inside he can't have a wish to be something else.

Apartment 4-D was at the far end of the first cross
corridor. I was halfway down the corridor when the
shots came from ahead. Three shots, the noise amplified
by the solid walls. The door to 4-D was ajar. I began to
run, bringing out my old pistol.

I stopped running—my pistol wasn't there. I had left
it in my bag in the car. I swore at myself and my crazy
dislike of guns. But I didn't swear hard. With a gun, I
might have charged into 4-D, a perfect target for a killer
who heard me coming. Without a gun, I went on carefully. I might lose time, and lose the killer, but that was
better than losing the whole game—the only game I
had, my life.

I pushed the door all the way open slowly. No one
shot. The apartment was dark as I went in. I heard a
faint sound somewhere at the rear. I walked through as
silently as I could, feeling naked without a gun. The rear
service door in the kitchen was open. I went out to the
back landing with my stomach in my toes. I listened,
and heard nothing at all.

That scared me. I had heard a sound, and now I
heard nothing. Was someone close and silent, breathing

hard but slow, waiting with a gun? I moved to the stairs through air that felt like a heavy wall.

Far below there was a faint sound—a door closing somewhere at the bottom of the service stairs. My quarry was gone. My stomach got lighter. I was some detective. A man with a gun had just escaped me, and I felt good. There's no exhilaration for me in danger, and when I'm let off the hook, I'm happy.

I went back inside, and found Carl Gans on the floor of a dark room hung with framed photos of fighters he had known. There was almost no blood. His chest oozed a little blood from three small holes no larger than a pencil. A .25- or .22-caliber gun. Bullets that size could hit a man ten times and cause no real damage. I kneeled down.

"Gans? Who was it? Can you hear me?"

He breathed hoarsely, blood liquid in his throat, but he breathed. I smelled the whisky—a lot of whisky. His single glass stood on a table beside a bottle. He had been drowning his loss of Zaremba. It explained how he had been surprised in his own apartment.

"Gans?" I said.

His eyes were closed. He didn't open them. He was in some other world, facing what neither of us could know, but already gone from this world where men like me asked questions and worried about who had shot him.

His lips barely moved as if he didn't want to make any movement. "Dark. Behind me. No face. Shot."

His voice was oddly clear, firm in its light, hoarse way, and still faintly slurring with the whisky in him. He didn't ask who I was. That made no difference to him now.

His lips moved, "Raul Negra. She asked about Negra. The Crawford kid, Raul Negra. October, fifty-seven. October tenth, fifty-seven. October tenth, fifty-seven. October—"

His breathing became irregular, with long and short

gaps. I waited for the next breath. It didn't come. He died without a sigh or a cough.

I stood up and went to call Captain Gazzo.

Gazzo sat in Carl Gans's lighted living room. I had told him all I'd learned. He already knew about my client. He was letting that pass. His men worked over Gans and the room.

"Gans worked for Abram Zaremba a long time," I said. "Now they're both dead. Gans was one of the men Francesca made a play for in New York. I came to ask questions. Maybe someone didn't want Gans to answer any questions. He was the last stop on her search for her father—maybe. Unless maybe Zaremba was. Maybe a lot of things. We don't know enough yet."

"Ralph Blackwind," Gazzo said. "I don't get many Indians, only those Mohawks over in Brooklyn when they go on a spree. So now we go through it again, check them all out: Harmon Dunstan, his wife, your client, the Bazer girl, the Crawfords, Frank Keefer, Joel Pender, the lot. Jonas'll be busy."

"Don't forget Anthony Sasser and Carter Vance."

"I won't forget them. What about my missing month?"

"Somewhere out west, I think," I said. "She had Indian jewelry when she had nothing else. Fifteen years is a long time, but the answer, for her and for us, has to be where Ralph Blackwind started. The beginning of the trail that led her to New York. Auburn Prison should have the information. Where he came from, his past."

"I'll get after it," Gazzo said. "Any guesses, Dan?"

"None. I'm charging down blind trails. At least there are some trails now."

The M.E. came up. "Three shots in his chest. Two knicked the heart. Bad luck. Could have missed just as easy, and then all he'd have had was an itch. Short range, a .22-caliber, probably a vest-pocket or purse gun. The bullets are still in him, no power to go through.

Two look in fine shape. Just find the gun to match, and you've got your man. Have fun."

The M.E. wasn't callous, only experienced. A man who lives where death delights every day has to find a way to stay working for his money. He walked away to tell his men to take the body, and Captain Gazzo stood up.

"I'll call when I have word," Gazzo said to me.

It was a dismissal. Gazzo wanted to get his mind back to the slow, tedious routine that solves most cases. I didn't think it would solve this one. Neither did he. He looked at his men who were working on the room without much hope.

I went down to my car, and drove home. When I got there, I tried calling Marty again. No answer. It had been a lonely two weeks for me. I cooked myself some dinner—hamburger and peas with too much bread. Then I went to bed. The drug, my bruises, and the bullet furrow in my head had caught up to me.

I lay thinking of Marty, and of Felicia Crawford out in the night somewhere, but there was no profit in any of that. So I thought of Muriel Roark and her muscular dancer's legs up in Dresden. It was a nice thought to sleep on.

CHAPTER NINETEEN

The telephone woke me up. The sun was up, and the wind from my open window was almost warm. October weather—winter and spring coming and going in autumn.

"Fortune," I said into the receiver, wishing for the ten-millionth time that I had two arms and could get a cigarette while holding a phone without the contortions I had to go through one move at a time, the phone tucked under my chin.

"Gazzo, Dan. Got a pencil and paper?"

I gave up on the cigarette, got the pencil and paper.

"Go ahead, Captain," I said.

"Ralph Blackwind was born at the Pine River Agency, Pine River, Arizona, on July 12, 1929. Lived there until he went into the army in April 1950. Want the prison report?"

"I'd like to hear the official version, yes."

"Convicted of assault-with-intent-to-murder, December 1953, sent to Auburn. Difficult prisoner, bad record of fights. He escaped with three others in October 1956. A prison guard was killed. Two prisoners were killed, one apprehended fast, but not Blackwind. The surviving prisoner stated Blackwind was drowned in a lake. No body found at first, intensive all-states manhunt continued for months without any trace of Blackwind. Body finally located in lake that matched Blackwind every way that could be matched. Search for him continued less intensively for two more years. Declared officially dead in 1959."

I was silent, "It sounds pretty convincing."

"Yeh, it does, but you never can be sure without a positive body all the way," Gazzo said. "At the time of his escape, his known relatives were his father, Two Bears Walk Near, at the Pine River Agency; a brother, John Two Bears, also Pine River Agency; and a sister, Woman Of Two Bears, Pine River Agency. They were all checked out and watched. His friends too."

"Where is Pine River?"

"In southeast Arizona. Nearest town is Fort Johns, about six hundred people strong. Nearest big cities are Flagstaff, and Gallup, New Mexico. Phoenix is the only real city near, after that it's covered wagons. The Agency itself is a small reservation, maybe two hundred people on a lot of land. Apache, the Indian people say, but they admit the names sound more like Navajo."

"What about our suspects and Carl Gans's killing?"

"Most of them have no alibis. Only Anthony Sasser, and I wonder about him. He was close to Zaremba, stands to cash-in on Zaremba's holdings, and has the only real alibi. Not even your client, John Andera, has one this time. We'll follow up."

His voice wasn't optimistic. Somehow, a big piece was missing—the key piece. Maybe it was out in Arizona.

"I guess I take a jet," I said.

"Take your snake-bite kit, too," Gazzo said, and hung up.

Now I had my cigarette. I didn't want to go to Pine River, or even to Phoenix. I'm a city man. But I called, and got a seat on a jet that left for Phoenix in two hours.

We're a homogeneous nation now, and Phoenix has culture and country club suburbs where the middle-class rich throw parties just like those of East Orange or Bridgeport. The automobile began the homogenizing, the movies carried it ahead, and the jet and TV completed the process. The rough pattern of misshaped grits we used to be is smoothed into a thin gruel from one end of the bowl to the other, sugared by comfort.

I went right out on a smaller plane to Flagstaff, and hired a car there. I drove out east along route 66, and the difference came to meet me. Outside Phoenix the land was still there—the "west" they know even in Vladivostok. A dry land of buff-and-red-ocher color with its wiry gray brush; the long, flat mesas; the red cliffs; the high blue sky bleached almost white by the sun. You could still imagine the yipping bark of the Cheyenne and Apache riding down on the wind and dust. A strong wind, blowing the dust, and a feeling of winter that would pile snow like a sheet of lava here. A snow that would isolate the Indians and ranchers for months sometimes, and only their knowledge, and today the helicopter, would keep them alive. A barren, dead land where no one should live, and our largesse to the Indians. If it could grow even grass, we'd steal it.

I turned off on highway 77, and then onto a blacktop county road through the one-street town of Fort Johns, and finally into the town of Pine River that didn't even have a street. It was a ragged double row of adobe shacks and hogans along the blacktop road. Dry dirt yards were littered with pieces of broken machines and cast-out appliances. There was a flat-roofed adobe restaurant festooned with signs, and a single one-pump gas station facing it across the highway. The blacktop road led straight as an arrow between the shacks, and vanished into a completely empty distance.

I parked at the restaurant. Indians sat against its walls. They wore jeans, sheepskin jackets, and broad-brimmed white stetsons—all identical except for their boots. Behind the restaurant some Indian women sat in a circle, wearing the voluminous, decorated Indian dresses with long, full skirts. Two younger girls stood apart from them wearing jeans and shirts like the men. The older women ignored them.

Inside the restaurant two men ate at a long counter, both Indians. The woman behind the counter was also Indian.

"I'm looking for the Pine River Agency," I said.

"Why?" she said.

"I want to find a man named Two Bears Walk Near."

"He's an old man. He might be dead. I don't know."

"I'll find out," I said.

"You're looking for the two women? Only one of them's there now. The other left."

"How do I get there?" I said.

"Two Bears Walk Near is very old. A chief, if we had any chiefs anymore. You want his son, John Two Bears."

"I want Ralph Blackwind," I said.

She wiped her hands on the old skirt she wore. "You go a mile south, a gravel road to the left. Two miles in is the trading post."

One of the men who had been eating got up and went out without paying. I followed him out. The Indian crossed the highway to the gas station and went inside the office. I got into my rented car, and drove the mile to the gravel road. A battered sign read: Pine River Agency.

The gravel road rattled my teeth all the way. It was full of holes and boulders I had to drive around. It wound down through deep arroyos until there was no more sign of the highway behind me, or of any life I knew. I was back in another century. Smoke seemed to rise out of the rocks themselves in the distance, no buildings in sight. Until I came over a rise and saw a rocky valley on the banks of a dry river bed. There was a rambling adobe building with a sign: Trading Post, Pine River Agency. A few smaller adobe shacks, and some hogans, were scattered up the slopes of the valley with a few pinto ponies and two good horses wandering among them.

I parked and went into the trading post. A tall Caucasian sat at a desk behind a store counter. He was alone, and I realized that I had seen no one in the whole small valley.

"I'm looking for Two Bears Walk Near," I said.

"He's old," the man said without turning.

He was adding a column of figures. They didn't seem to add to what he wanted, so he began to add them again.

"Also Ralph Blackwind," I said.

"You're late," he said.

"I usually am, but I try."

He turned and looked me over. "Good for you."

"Thanks," I said. "Did Ralph Blackwind ever come home?"

"Naturally," he said. "An Indian always comes home to the land."

"Naturally," I said.

"Their spirits return," he said.

He hadn't even looked at my missing arm. He turned back to his column of figures, began to add them again.

"Where do I find Two Bears Walk Near? I know he's an old man. It's all right."

"You listen," he said.

"Then say something," I said, as two people walked in the trading post door. A man and a woman.

He was a small Indian with long hair held by a hairband. Perhaps twenty-four, he wore the same Levi's, jacket and cowboy boots. The woman also wore jeans, but the kind from Saks-Fifth, and her sheepskin jacket was too big for her: Felicia Crawford. Now I knew what that Indian in Pine River had done in the gas station office—called them here at the agency.

"Hello, Felicia," I said.

"This is Paul Two Bears," Felicia said. "My cousin."

"Dan Fortune," I said, and held out my hand.

He didn't take it. "You had a long trip," he said.

"Not if I get some answers," I said.

Felicia said, "Francesca was here for two weeks that first month, Mr. Fortune. She told me in her first note. Just that it was wonderful here, a great moment, she knew who we were. So I came to see."

"That's all she said? All you knew? Not about your father?"

"Not then, no."

"Now you know," I said. "What else did Francesca learn?"

The young Indian, Paul Two Bears, said, "She talked to my grandfather. He says he'll talk to you too. Come on."

I followed them out. The man at the desk was still adding his column of figures. I had the feeling that he would sit and add all winter until he got the answer he needed, or until the answer was so obsolete it could be forgotten. He didn't look discouraged. He sat back, lighted a cigarette, and considered what to do next to make the figures add to what he needed.

Paul Two Bears and Felicia led me down a worn path, and across the dry river bed. Nothing grew anywhere. The only animals were the horses. There were no electric lines, no gas pipes, and the only telephone line reached the trading post and stopped there.

"Is there ever water in the river?" I asked.

"Sometimes," Paul Two Bears said.

Felicia said, "When the white ranchers upriver open their dams because they have too much water. The whole river is dammed, the ranchers own the water. They'll kill any man who tries to get it from them, make them share with the Indians."

"How many Indians are there here?"

"In the area, thousands," Paul Two Bears said. "On the Agency just two hundred and ten. It's all ours." He laughed as he waved an arm to encompass the whole, barren countryside, and we climbed the opposite bank. The trail wore up over the rim of the valley, and down again into a narrow arroyo where three hogans clustered. We went into the middle hogan. An old man sat on rugs against the rear wall.

"This man has come to talk, Grandfather," Paul Two Bears said to the old man.

The old man was short and heavy. His dark brown eyes were alert in a face incredibly wrinkled and creased with ridges that looked as hard as rock. His face was the color of wet leather. He watched me with his lively eyes.

"About what you told my sister," Felicia said, and added, "Grandfather."

The word was awkward on her lips, strange to her, but eager, too. The old man smiled at her, and spoke to me:

"What I told her was for her."

He had a soft, clear voice with no real accent. An educated voice. He was dressed in older Indian clothes as if he had spent his life here, but his voice had been other places. I guessed that he was very old, as everyone said.

"She's dead," I said. "I want to find who killed her."

"Why?" he said.

"To know that the person won't kill anyone else."

The old man thought about it. "She was my granddaughter. It's good to find a granddaughter at my age. This one here is also my granddaughter. She is alive. Is there danger for her?"

"I don't know," I said. "There might be."

He nodded. "You want to know, but you must know already, or you would not be here."

"I guess, I don't know," I said. "Your granddaughter came looking for her father, your son, but what did she find?"

"Only she could have told you that."

"What had her other grandfather told her?"

"That my son was her true father."

"She knew that from someone else. Is your son alive?"

"Only my son knows if he lives," the old man said.

"Was he killed in the escape from prison fifteen years ago?" I said.

The old man sat for a time. He didn't close his eyes, but he wasn't seeing the interior of the hogan anymore. Then his old body seemed to sit straighter.

"My name is Two Bears Walk Near, I am ninety-six years old," he said, speaking lower but harder. "The white men do not know who I am, who we are. We live inside the invisible walls of our ways. The white men say they know who we are, but they don't, and that is good. What a white man knows he must take. He cannot help himself, it is his way to take. He took our land, our water, our freedom, and our life. He took our tribe. On the documents we are called Apache. We live as Navajo. We are one with all Indians. But we are really Comanche. A remnant lost when I was young, and the white men wrote us down as Apache, so we lost our past. They took our names, made them empty names. There was a Sioux once called Man Afraid Of His Horses. That was not his name. His name was—Young Men Are Afraid Of His Horses, because he was a greater trainer of horses that the enemy feared. But the white men stole his true name. In our language my son has a name—He Who Walked A Black Wind. His name was given on the day as a boy he dared to walk out alone toward a tornado while the rest of us hid. The white men made him 'Blackwind,' so stole his name. What no man can steal is his life. Each man alone knows his own life, knows if he lives or only walks."

Now he closed his eyes. Not because he was tired—I sensed that he could talk all day—but as if to listen to his own words again, and see if he had said it the way he wanted to. For him, conversation was a form of art, of literature.

"That is philosophy," I said. "I have to deal with the

smaller facts. A lost daughter wants to come home, wants a live father."

"Perhaps home is not a good place," the old man said, his eyes open again. "I'll tell you about my son. Another story. History this time, not philosophy, Mr. Fortune. At my age all I have are stories. Our stories are part of our whole lives, not separate works of art. There is no difference between a story and an event. Our stories are your facts, too."

His eyes remained open, but became distant again. "Many years ago when I was a very young man, perhaps fifteen, there was nothing here but our camp on the reservation. The nearest walls and white men were at Fort Johns. We young men were angry, violent. A lot of bad things had been done to us by the settlers and soldiers. Remember, this was 1890. The Apache were still free, still at war. We young men listened to the tales of the Apache, and we were angry to be men like them. So we planned a raid on Fort Johns.

"There were only thirty-five of us, but Old Nana had once terrorized all of the Southwest with only ten Apaches. We were Comanche, better than Apache. We were very brave, very young. So we prepared our raid. The old men were against us, but they were afraid to stop us, or even talk against us. Many of them were as foolish as we were. All but one old chief. In Council he stood up and spoke against us—we were fools, children; our weapons were useless; we hadn't fought in our lives; our whole small tribe hadn't fought for twenty years; we didn't know how to fight, or what war was like; the soldiers at Fort Johns were veterans; we wouldn't even get near the Fort unseen; the only way for our tribe to survive was to keep our ways and bide our time and stay away from the white man until there was a new day. That was what he said.

"And he said that if the Council did not stop us, he would do it alone. The Council failed to agree. The raid was to go on. That one old man got on his horse and started for Fort Johns. He told us that he would warn the soldiers. He rode off alone, so we killed him. Ten of us rode after him and killed him.

"That old man was my grandfather."

CHAPTER TWENTY

"The raid failed, of course, we were all killed or captured after a few shots. We went to prison, our tribe was severely punished, almost broken, and we have been poor and weak and forgotten here ever since. But that is not my story."

He was an artist in his way, that old man—an artist with words, the oral tradition of literature. In that hogan he had us all mesmerized, hanging on every word: Felicia, Paul Two Bears, myself. He spoke as a master writer writes, satisfying our simple need to know the end, to know what had happened, and then sweeping it away while holding us for his real story.

"My story," he said, "is honest anger turned to black rage. We young men had an honest anger then, but we let it become a dishonest rage inside us that let me kill my own grandfather. My son, He Who Walked a Black Wind, was the same in his time. He was a boy of honest anger, good for himself and the tribe, but the white man is intelligent, he knows by intuition how to dominate, enslave, weaken. The white man sent my son to war in Korea, took his anger and made it into a rage—a rage first against strangers, then against his own family, and then against life itself. Indians are communal, one with the land. White men are not, and my son in his rage lost the land and his past and became white. He took the ways of white men, the values, and it doomed him to his fate."

The old man made a sound in the hogan, maybe it was a sigh, I couldn't really tell. He had me paralyzed with the force of his flowing words. But he made some sound, and his voice became sad, almost tired.

"My son wanted to build among us, live with us with his wife. When she did not want this, his rage made him do the act that lost him his work with the land, and so lost him his life. A man's work is his soul. When I came from prison in my time, I too walked far from here. But I learned that you cannot defeat people by becoming as they are. I learned that my grandfather had been wise, and I came home to wait for our time, to keep our ways ready. My son came from prison a white man, driftwood on an empty river."

A master, the old man, bringing us all back into the hogan and the present by his change of voice, his own return to a tone that was tired and normal and in the present.

I said, "But he is alive? Somewhere?"

"He still walks," the old man said. "I don't know where."

"You told Francesca that?"

"Her other grandfather had already told her. A letter from my son had come to him years ago. The white grandfather perhaps liked my son, he did not tell what he knew."

"But he told Francesca, and she came here. What did you tell her?"

"That my son did not die from that prison. Many months after, he came here. The police had been here, had looked, and had not found him. He was a man who knew the land and the wind. He came home without being seen by anyone, but he did not stay. He knew he could not stay here. He left in the night as he had come. Once he wrote from Los Angeles, and once from the place of a man he had known in the army."

"Harmon Dunstan? His captain?"

"That was the man."

"This was all fifteen years ago?"

He nodded. "Later, the money began. It came without words or name, but I knew he sent it. A lot of money each time. The money has been good, but granddaughters are better. I found two new granddaughters. I am glad."

The old man stood up, almost without effort, and walked out of the hogan. No one followed him. I heard a horse walk slowly away toward the higher mesas. He was a strong old man. I looked at the young Indian, Paul Two Bears.

"Harmon Dunstan, and L.A., that's all she knew?"

"That's all we know here," Paul Two Bears said.

"What about that money?"

Felicia said, "It came at irregular intervals. The first time in October 1957. Maybe fifteen times since. A lot of money, at least five thousand dollars each time. No pattern."

"But no more letters. As if he was making money, but was ashamed of it, or afraid to reveal himself to anyone?"

"I don't know why," Felicia said.

"He'd murdered a prison guard, Felicia," I said, "and he was supposed to be dead. He had to hide. But his people here wouldn't have told on him. So why not write?"

She was silent. I thought about it. A whole new identity, maybe, and afraid to risk even a letter to Pine River? The date of that first letter with money crawled in my mind—October 1957. Where had I heard it? Then it came to me—Carl Gans! The bouncer's dying words—October, fifty-seven. Over and over.

"How long have you been here, Felicia?" I asked.

"Since the night I saw you. They wouldn't talk to me at first, until I proved who I was."

"You've been here ever since?"

Paul Two Bears said, "She has been here. She didn't leave."

He had guessed why I wanted to know even though I

hadn't mentioned Abram Zaremba or Carl Gans yet. But what did it prove? That they would lie for her, or that it was true, take your pick.

"I like it here," Felicia said. "I feel at home."

"Francesca told you she liked it here, but she left."

Paul Two Bears said, "Francesca was more restless, she had to find her father. We told her that my uncle was a lost man, that he wouldn't even want her to find him. She had to look."

"You don't, Felicia?" I said.

"I don't know. It's not so important to me, I guess. Fran felt more rejected by Mother than I did, more lost in Dresden."

"How much do you know about what happened in Dresden eighteen years ago? When your father came for all of you?"

"Only what they know here. Tell me, Mr. Fortune."

I told her. I also told her about the murders of Abram Zaremba and Carl Gans. Her eyes grew wider, and darker, and more afraid. When I finished, she said:

"All because Fran was looking for our father?"

"I don't know that," I said.

"Her scar," she said. "Shot because of our father. I remember the nightmares. As if, somehow, Fran remembered it more. The shock of the wound in her memory, maybe."

"Maybe," I said.

She said, "What did happen to Fran, Mr. Fortune?"

"There are a lot of possibilities still," I said. "She went to Harmon Dunstan, and then she moved on. I think she picked up a fifteen-year-old trail. The trail of a man supposed to be dead, and with a prison guard murder hanging over his head. A fugitive, Felicia, hiding one way or another. How would he know who she was? Just some girl trailing him. And even if he did know her, what could she have meant to him by now?"

"You think he . . . ? To stay hidden? No!"

"Maybe her murder was more to do with Abram

Zaremba, and the lawyer Mark Leland, and the Black Mountain Lake project, after all. I don't know," I said. "Or there could be someone else who doesn't want Ralph Blackwind found."

Felicia said, "I'm afraid. Afraid to know."

"We'll have to find him before we know anything," I said. I looked at Paul Two Bears. "What does he look like, Two Bears?"

"I never saw him," the youth said. He took a small snapshot from his jacket. "My father had this picture. It's our only one, and it's twenty years old or more."

It was a photo of a youth in Levi's, boots and stetson, standing beside a pinto pony. The wide brim shaded his face, and it was hard to tell how dark he was. Beside the horse, he seemed about five-feet-seven-or-eight, and his skin was shining smooth. He resembled none of the men I knew in the case, but twenty hard years had passed. A lot had happened to Ralph Blackwind, but you can usually see the man of forty in the youth of twenty-two or so.

Usually, but not always, no. Some men change a great deal between twenty and forty, especially with hard living and weight, and the young Indian in the photo was whip thin. Still, if he was anyone I knew, there should have been a hint at least, a feeling. Unless—?

"Was his face changed by the war, or later?"

"Not the war so much, my father said, but by his escape from North Korea, and by prison later," Paul Two Bears said. "The escape changed his whole expression, and his face was beaten in prison fights. My father said he was badly scarred in the prison break, too."

No one I knew in the case had serious scars. I thought about all the money he had sent to Pine River. A man with a lot of money, scars on his face, and a need to hide.

"Was he very dark?"

"No, his mother was half-Caucasian," Paul Two

Bears said. "My grandfather's last wife. Ralph was born when the old man was fifty-four. His hair wasn't black, either. Dark brown, going gray even fifteen years ago, my father said."

"What color eyes?"

"Dark brown, like all of us."

I nodded. "All right, I'll go back and see if I can follow Francesca's trail. You want to stay here, Felicia?"

She thought, looked around the inside of the hogan. "No, I'll go back with you. I suppose I want to know, and I want my mother and fath . . . Dad Crawford, to know what I've found here. Later, maybe . . . I can come back."

Paul Two Bears said, "I'll come with you."

That was the way we left Pine River, the three of us.

CHAPTER TWENTY-ONE

We landed at Kennedy early in the cold afternoon. I walked Felicia and Paul Two Bears to their Allegheny Airlines flight for Dresden. I didn't ask her what she planned, or give her any advice. I had a hunch she already knew her plans. She wasn't a halfway girl anymore.

I caught a taxi to Forty-second and Fifth Avenue— the Main Library. I got the microfilm for The *New York Times* for the whole month of October 1957. Carl Gans had named a date, too, as he died—October tenth. I ran the film through the viewer. The story was on page three on October eleventh, as I realized Carl Gans had known it was. Trying to tell me fast at the end.

An attempted holdup, that might have been more of an attempted business extortion, had been foiled the night before at the Emerald Room by the heroic action of one Raul Negra, a kitchen helper. (That was the name Carl Gans had used, had said that Francesca had asked about—Raul Negra.)

Four men had entered the restaurant just at closing time. They shot the bouncer, Carl Gans, in the leg, killed a bodyguard of the owner, Commissioner Abram Zaremba, lined up the staff, and started to smash the place and rob the registers. Raul Negra, unseen in the kitchen, had crawled out unobserved by the gunmen, picked up the dead bodyguard's gun, and started shooting. With incredible skill and accuracy, the *Times* said, Negra used the tables as cover, and shot down all four of the gunmen without being scratched himself.

The police commended Negra, who was a Mexican

national and spoke no English, and who said he had learned to shoot in the Mexican army. Commissioner Zaremba, whose lawyer spoke for the hero, rewarded the man with an immediate ten thousand dollars, and a better position in his Chicago office. That was all, and though I looked at every issue for another month, there was no further mention of heroic Raul Negra. He seemed to have faded away—I bet he had, and fast.

I didn't doubt who Raul Negra had really been, or why he spoke no English to the police, and had Zaremba's lawyers talk for him. He had acted the way a trained, experienced soldier would have, using all the skills learned in a hard war, and all the skills of an Indian who had crossed two thousand miles of populated country without once being seen, or even suspected, by the police—the same way the Apache Masai had not so very long ago.

The reward money coincided exactly with the first money that arrived at Pine River. I wondered what else Abram Zaremba had done for "Raul Negra." A job, the newspaper said, but what job, and had it been in Chicago? Or had Ralph Blackwind used the rest of that ten thousand dollars to repair, and heavily change, his scarred face, and work a lot closer to Dresden and New York?

The Dunstan house was as I had left it days before, except that one car was gone. I parked my rerented car, and walked up to the door for the third time. This time, Harmon Dunstan opened the door himself.

"Don't you ever stop, Fortune?"

"When it's finished. The police checked you out for the murder of Carl Gans?"

"Yes. I had no alibi, neither did Grace. She's not home."

"I don't want her," I said, and pushed him back into that polished living room. He was small, and dark, but strong enough. "You knew Carl Gans, didn't you?"

"I never met him, no."

"But you met Raul Negra. Fifteen years ago."

He went to the bar, poured his inevitable drink.

I said, "When did Ralph Blackwind become Raul Negra?"

Dunstan looked for a cigarette. I let him look. There was no hurry. He was going to have to talk now.

"It's not scandal you were scared about, or even involvement," I said. "It was hiding an escaped prisoner who had killed a prison guard, and maybe the man found in the Catskill lake, too. He came to his old captain—who maybe owed him a big favor or two."

It was a guess in the dark, but it was the key that opened him up. I had guessed right.

"He saved my life twice in Korea," Dunstan said, the words coming in a rush now, as if pent up since the night Francesca Crawford had died. "He came here five months after he escaped. He'd been lucky, he said, a freak fluke that they just about believed he was dead, and he was able to work his way back to Pine River like a ghost the way he had made it out of North Korea. He never told me just what had happened, but he'd realized that when it took the police so long to find that body in the lake, they couldn't be sure just who it was in the lake. He had a real chance, as long as he made no mistakes. That's why he left Pine River, he could be found there.

"He went to L.A., but was nearly spotted. So he got fake Mexican papers as Raul Negra, and came to me. The police had been around to me a lot, I didn't think they'd come again, and I owed Ralph. I gave him a job in my stockroom. But the police did come again, and Ralph decided it was too risky, and left. I haven't seen or heard from him since—almost fifteen years. I don't regret what I did, but I'd hidden a fugitive murderer, and I've been scared ever since the Crawford girl came around and then was killed."

He gulped at his drink. "What I did was a crime. I've

worked too hard and long to build my business. I won't lose it. It's all I have."

"You've got a wife, too, but you chase women."

"A wife, but no woman," Dunstan said. "Maybe that was why I helped Ralph then, too. He'd had a raw deal from a woman. But he was a man, he fought. I never could. I've got a good business, lots of money, a good home, but I had no luck with my woman, not even back then, and there's nothing I could ever do about it."

He sat down on a bar stool. "You see, I love Grace. I always have. I want her, but she never wanted me—not the way I want her to want me. She makes a good home, a comfortable life. A good companion and hostess, and nothing else."

At another time I might have had something to say about his troubles, about his wife and him. But if he was telling the truth, he wasn't important to me now. He didn't count.

"What did Blackwind look like then?" I said.

"Older. His jaw had been broken, scars on his face, his hair blackened, his skin very dark to look Mexican. I barely knew him. He spoke Spanish except to me."

"Where did he go after he left your job?"

Dunstan licked at his lips. "I sent him to Zaremba."

He didn't look at me now. "All right, I lied. I was Zaremba's investment counselor for ten years. I broke with him six years ago. I haven't even talked to him since. But when he was killed too, I was scared, and I lied."

"Did Carl Gans know you'd sent Ralph Blackwind to Zaremba?"

"I don't know. I never knew what happened to Ralph, or what job Zaremba gave him. I didn't want to."

"Kitchen helper, for a time at least," I said. "What else have you lied about, Dunstan? Were you spying on Francesca?"

"Not spying, hanging around like a hungry damned puppy. I was ashamed to tell, and scared, too." He looked at me. "I was watching her place that night, watching for men, you know? Like a sick adolescent!"

"Did you see any men?"

"Yes. Around eight P.M. A tall, blond guy maybe thirty. He met her on the street in front of the building, and he went up with her. He was there over an hour. He didn't come back while I was watching. I gave up around eleven P.M."

"You didn't go up yourself?"

"No! I swear I didn't!"

"Next time tell it, save yourself a week of worrying."

"Next time? No next time. Not for me. I know now."

He was right. For him, the rest would be repetition. I started for the living room door, and met Grace Dunstan on her way in. I nodded to her, but I didn't speak. I had nothing to ask her that she would tell me.

She put down some packages, took the drink Dunstan gave her, and they sat side by side on the bar stools. Neither of them spoke. Yet I sensed that if either of them went away, the other would crack open with emptiness. They had little together, but nothing at all apart.

I went out to my car.

I drove toward the city, and thought about the Dunstans. There are many kinds of marriages, and most of them not the kind made by the simple people without problems who never lived except in the shiny pages of women's magazines. The Dunstans had no real marriage at all, yet there was something that held them together like a vise.

I stopped at a pay booth to call John Andera's office. He was there. I told him to meet me at my office, and he was waiting when I arrived. We went up to my office.

"You have something to report, Fortune?" Andera said.

His face was composed, but his hands were tense, and his cloudy blue eyes watched me like a man who wants to hear an answer, and yet doesn't because he won't really like it.

"Francesca was in New York looking for her real father," I said, and told him everything I had learned. "Did you know Ralph Blackwind, or Raul Negra fifteen years ago? Did she ask about either of them?"

"Her real father?" he said, and that stunned look came back into his eyes, maybe thinking that Francesca hadn't been interested in him at all, had used him. "No, I never knew any Ralph Blackwind, or Raul Negra. I'm sure. But . . . yes, she did mention a Raul Negra. I remember now. It was casual, you know? We were talking about minority employment, and she wondered if my company hired Mexicans. She said she knew a Raul Negra who had worked for us. I didn't know about him."

"Who owns Marvel Office Equipment?" I said.

"Two or three men."

"Is one of them Abram Zaremba? Or was he an owner?"

"Yes, he had a minority interest. I never met him."

Abram Zaremba. The trail of Ralph Blackwind seemed to lead all around him. The trail and the murders. And if it all led to Zaremba, it led to Dresden too —or somewhere close.

I said, "Francesca did three things—she opposed the Black Mountain Lake project in Dresden, she saw the man who killed Mark Leland, and she went looking for her real father. Two of those things seem to go straight to Abram Zaremba, and I think Mark Leland will lead to Zaremba too.

"Her real father is a fugitive, a wanted killer, who is safe because he's supposed to be dead. Francesca knew he was alive, and started looking for him, turning over old rocks. As far as we know, the last time he saw her was eighteen years ago when she was under three. Would he know her? Would he care if he did? A fugitive whose safety was staying 'dead'?"

I let Andera think about that. He thought, and he had that man-hit-by-a-train look again. "Her father? You think that's possible, Fortune?"

"Fear can make monsters out of even simple people, and most of us aren't simple," I said. "Or she could have seen more than she told the night Mark Leland was killed. She could have known something bad about the Black Mountain Lake project. I don't know, but one of those things killed her, or maybe they're all tied together, all really one thing.

"They all seem to focus on Abram Zaremba, and he was killed, too. Ralph Blackwind's trail ends at Abram Zaremba. Anthony Sasser, that businessman friend of the Crawfords who was put on the crime commission, and who tailed me and beat me up in New York, worked with Abram Zaremba, and was close to Francesca. Mayor Martin Crawford worked with Zaremba, too. So both of Francesca's 'fathers' were in Abram Zaremba's orbit. Maybe it's all cause and effect. No matter what killed Francesca, the chain began when she was approached by Mark Leland. He went to her because she was Mayor Crawford's daughter, and Crawford was tied to Abram Zaremba's scheme for Black Mountain Lake, but the result was that she learned she had a real father."

John Andera looked past me at the fine view of the air-shaft wall outside the one window of my office.

"What will you do, then?" he said.

"Report Ralph Blackwind to the police. Now that they know he's alive, they'll find him. I think he'll be somewhere around Abram Zaremba's organization. I think he's been close to Zaremba for fifteen years. I think he'll be found now, but I hope we're in time."

"In time?" Andera said.

"Carl Gans and Zaremba may not be the last victims. They weren't in Dresden when Mark Leland died, and they didn't know Francesca. If she knew more about Leland's death than she told, someone else must have found that out and fingered her, and that someone must know who killed her."

"You know who?" Andera said.

"Not yet, but I will," I said, and added, "Then there's Felicia Crawford. She's following the same trail Francesca did, and that might make her a target too."

Andera said, "Then you better hurry."

"I'll hurry," I said. "After I get my expenses."

I gave him the expense account I'd worked up on the jet from Phoenix. He paid it without asking a question, it was only padded a little. After he'd gone, I counted the money for a time. I was tired. I didn't feel like moving. There are some cases that leave me feeling low as they inexorably unravel like a ball of yarn dropped from a tall building. Like watching a movie where a mob hangs an innocent man. You know the mob will be punished later, but what good does that do the dead man? You walk away feeling cheated. It's all wrong.

But I called Gazzo, told him about Arizona. He would go to work finding Ralph Blackwind. So would I.

CHAPTER TWENTY-TWO

It was just dark when I arrived in Dresden again, and a rain had begun. A slow rain, silent and without wind, that dripped from the bare trees. The flowers around the small-time playboy Frank Keefer's house were sodden.

Celia Bazer answered my ring. "They're inside," she said.

Her eye was still bruised, and I wanted to ask her why she stayed, but she wouldn't really have an answer. Because we all need something or someone, and at least Frank Keefer was a good man when the lights were out, and that was better than a man who was good nowhere. She read my mind. It's not hard.

She touched her eye. "He's nice most of the time. He's always disappointed, and then I'm here, and he lets me help him. He'll support me, and he'll stick, even if he strays sometimes. When his schemes blow up, he runs to me. We've got each other."

They had each other, and the Dunstans had everything but. Take your choice, find the miracle of both at once, settle for a little of each, or live alone. It usually works out.

Frank Keefer and his uncle, Joel Pender, were in the living room. Pender watched the TV morosely, and Keefer sat alone with a beer. All the mimeographed throwaways were still piled everywhere, and the mimeograph machine was covered and dusty.

"What happened to the throwaway scheme?" I asked.

"We printed them wrong, no one would pay," Keefer said, shrugged. "Joel had the wrong sale date, we were a day late getting them out. Who could use them? We spent the advances, no one'll pay us for another try. What the hell."

There was no fight in Frank Keefer for the moment. Joel Pender was put together with different glue. His thin shoulders were squared where he watched TV, as if prepared to go on undaunted—something good would still come along.

I said, "You came from out west, Pender?"

"Wyoming. The other side of nowhere."

"You came here less than fifteen years ago?"

"I forget," he said.

I let it go for the moment, turned to Frank Keefer.

"You lied again about New York and Francesca, Keefer," I said. "You met her, talked to her. You were seen."

He drank some beer. "Okay, I saw her. I tried once more for her, she threw me out. That's all."

"No," I said. "You're not a fool, you knew you had no chance when she dropped you up here. You went down there because you and Pender were scared of what Pender had told her when he was drunk. You'd been trying to find out where she was to be sure she wouldn't tell where she'd found out about her real father. You were scared of what the Mayor would do."

I turned on Joel Pender. "You have a hold on Mayor Crawford, right? It's what got you the city jobs. But you blurted it out to Francesca that night. What did you really tell her, Pender? Just that she wasn't Crawford's daughter, and who her real father was, isn't enough to give you a hold on the Mayor."

Celia Bazer and Keefer watched me and Pender. Keefer looked like he was enjoying watching Joel Pender squirm now.

I said, "I can tell Crawford you told the girl."

Joel Pender was a man who never gave up. In a way I had to admire the tenacity of the little man.

"A deal? If I tell you, you keep quiet all the way?"

"All right," I said. I didn't think it mattered much.

Pender swore. "I was here long before fifteen years, more like twenty. In those days I gardened for old Emil Van Hoek. I knew Katje. She come home in 1950 with her tail down and her belly up. The Van Hoeks wanted her to stick with the Indian, make a go for the kids. Katje wasn't having none of that, no sir. She wanted her share of the goodies. She took up with Crawford. He'd known her as a kid, but there was a big difference between a seventeen-year-old Van Hoek, and an eighteen-year-old married woman with twins. Crawford made his pitch, Katje said whoopee, but there was a problem, right?"

"She was married, had twins," I said. "You can get an annulment with children if you try early enough, but it wasn't easy even then."

"Right, so they had to fake it and fix it all the way," Pender said. "The Van Hoeks wouldn't help, said they'd even fight it. That would have stopped it for sure. So Crawford moved it away to Utica, faked residence and witnesses, and fixed the judge, too. I was a witness for them. We all swore the Indian ran out on Katje *before* he was sent to Korea, swore he reneged on wanting kids, hinted she'd been alone long enough so the twins weren't his. It worked, and that was my hold on Crawford. I mean, the fraud could be blown like tissue any time, all the sworn dates and facts were wrong."

"The Van Hoeks kept quiet after opposing it?"

"Katje didn't tell them until after she married Crawford. That left the Van Hoeks in a bind. If they talk, they hit Katje with fraud and bigamy. So what could they do?"

"Why did Crawford and Katje do it? Why not wait?"

"I figure Katje told Crawford no fun until the ring. I guess he couldn't wait, right? I figure she was afraid he'd slip away to some eager broad in Albany. I think she was scared of the Indian, too, and didn't want to wait and tell him she was through when he came back. I figure she thought if it was all done, she was remarried, he wouldn't kick up a bad fuss for the reason the Van Hoeks didn't—it would get Katje in real trouble."

It was a good point. A man might fight if he came home and was asked for a divorce at once. But how many young men, in reality married only a few months and separated for years, would cause trouble against a *fait accompli* for children they'd never known, and a woman who was already with another man? And passion makes people do many things, take risks.

"That's what you knew?" I said. "All of it?"

"That's enough," Pender said, "especially after they used the Indian's caper against Katje and the girls to make him keep quiet, too. The Indian could have crucified them all the way, in and out of court, if he hadn't shot old Emil Van Hoek. I mean, he was Katje's real husband still, right, with the annulment a fraud? Only he shot Emil Van Hoek, and that made it a felony-kidnapping, and gave Crawford the weapon to send the cops after them. When the Indian was caught, Crawford could make a deal—he'd defend the Indian, get the kidnapping charge dropped, if the Indian kept quiet about the annulment."

Pender reached for Frank Keefer's beer, took a drink, wiped his thin mouth. "What would you of done? I guess the Indian didn't care by then, and kidnapping got the chair, at least life. With him shooting old Van Hoek, the annulment fraud wasn't going to help him if Katje swore he'd taken her and the kids by force, with a gun. So he went along, and they got all the charges dropped except the lesser one for shooting old Van Hoek. That they couldn't drop all the way, and it sent the Indian up."

"You told Francesca all of that?"

"I told her, damn me, and Frank went down to try to make sure she kept quiet about where she heard it. Crawford never wanted it to come out, even if the Indian is dead."

"No," I said. "The Indian isn't dead, Pender."

The dark, scrawny man blinked like an owl. "Not dead? You're crazy. He got killed in that prison break."

"No," I said. "That's what old Emil Van Hoek told Francesca—Ralph Blackwind hadn't been killed fifteen years ago. Blackwind had written him once, maybe feeling bad about the shooting, who knows? The old man never told until Francesca came to him with your story. It was like bowling pins, Pender. Once the first one fell, they all came down. You blew it open."

Pender didn't speak. His thin face looked as if he couldn't speak. He was thinking about Mayor Crawford, and his future, and that his drunken anger had started a chain that had led to Francesca Crawford's death. If it had. Maybe he was thinking more about a live Indian, a real father, and a dead daughter.

"Alive?" Frank Keefer said. "Fran was looking for him, and she knew about the fake annulment? I mean—"

"Blackwind knew about the annulment eighteen years ago," I said. "You're both sure that was all Francesca knew? What did she say about her father when you saw her the day she died, Keefer?"

"That I could get lost for good, that she'd found her real dad's trail. She didn't say he was alive, but she said that someone was watching her. That was why she moved in with Celia. She didn't know who was watching her, but that businessman pal of Mayor Crawford's, Tony Sasser, had come to talk to her."

"Anthony Sasser talked to Francesca in New York!?"

Keefer nodded. "She said he came to bring her home, but she told him she was looking for her real father—that was her home."

"When was Sasser there? Damn it, why didn't you tell that sooner! *When* was he there?"

"Maybe a week before she got killed," Keefer said. "And I don't get mixed with Tony Sasser, no sir. I live here."

I went out of there fast.

But before I left, I saw the look on Joel Pender's face that told me that the uncle didn't think that any of them were going to do much living in Dresden anymore. On my way, I passed all those piles of useless mimeographed sheets. All a day late. It would always be a day late for Frank Keefer and Joel Pender, and they lived in perpetual fear—the fear of failure.

Celia Bazer had a fear too—the opposite fear. It was there in her eyes—the fear that Frank Keefer might lose *his* fear, that he might succeed some day. He was hers only in his failure, the failure her only insurance that he would always need her.

My fear was Anthony Sasser.

CHAPTER TWENTY-THREE

The Crawford mansion was alight through the trees in the steady rain. I parked in front. A maid opened the door, took me into the living room. The Crawfords were there, both of them—Katje Crawford in a dark red slack suit that suited her lean body, and Crawford drinking.

"Felicia was here," Crawford said. "She told us."

"Is she still here?"

"No. She went to a motel with that young Indian," he said, and shook his head. "It's almost impossible to believe."

I said, "That Ralph Blackwind's alive after you both tried to bury him eighteen years ago?"

Katje Crawford sat up straight. "He attacked us. He almost got the girls killed. He shot my father. I had a right to my own life. We had made a mistake, he should have seen that. Instead, he went crazy, and afterwards Martin defended him, got him less punishment than he deserved."

"You cut him out of your big life like a wart," I said. "The annulment was a cheat and a fix. Crawford had the money and power to do it. You fixed everyone, but Blackwind came home, and you had to fix him somehow. Your hands were dirty, and he could sink you, but you were lucky—he did a stupid trick, and he shot your father. So Crawford made a deal. Some deal! You got silence and your fine, rich life, and Blackwind got ten-to-twenty years in prison! A kid who'd just spent two years in a prison camp, was half out of his mind, couldn't take more prison so flipped and made a break, killed a guard, and finished himself. Only he fooled you, he didn't die."

Crawford was up, pacing, and I saw that ineffectuality in him again. There was a kind of anguish in his fleshy face, as if he was seeing himself eighteen years ago, younger and running fast with ambition.

"He didn't care, Fortune," he said. "I made the deal, yes, and it wasn't fair, but he didn't care, and what else could I do? I remember he said, 'Katje wants you, not me. That's it. Take her.' Could I let it all ruin everything we had, all we would be? The children too? I swear to you that I got him the lightest sentence anyone could have under the circumstances. He'd shot Emil Van Hoek, almost killed him."

Katje Crawford smoothed her slim red slacks. Her face was like stone, and yet there was conflict in her eyes, as if she was remembering not only the trouble eighteen years ago, but also those good months in New York over twenty years ago.

"He talked about the communal ranch we would build out in Arizona by getting water from the white ranchers," she said. "He wanted to take me to that wilderness of snakes. Sometimes a person doesn't know what he or she wants until suddenly the choice is there. I realized I wanted Dresden, with all the comfort and privileges that meant. When I found I was pregnant, I was doubly sure. My children raised in a hogan among lizards? No!"

I said, "The girls you were so close to? Never too busy with your privileges to mother them?"

She took a cigarette from another of her jade boxes, lit it. "We don't always know how things will turn out, Mr. Fortune, and don't judge me! I corrected a mistake, and I needed the annulment to make sure of Martin. I wanted to marry at once, settle it, and that annulment bound us together even more—we were both guilty of fraud and bribery. What happened later wasn't our fault."

"No, he played into your hands," I said. "He was a violent man, and he probably still is. Maybe more violent now. You must have been really scared when you found out he was alive, and maybe not so far away."

"Afraid? Why?" Katje Crawford said. "If he is alive, he hasn't come near us for fifteen years. Why would he now?"

Crawford said, "We didn't know he was alive until Felicia told us tonight. How could we have known?"

"Because Anthony Sasser found Francesca in New York a few weeks ago, and she told him."

"Sasser?" Martin Crawford said. "Found Francesca?"

"He talked to her. She told him she was looking for her real father, so you had to know then that Blackwind was alive."

"No," Crawford said. "Sasser never told us. No."

The big Mayor looked at his wife. Katje Crawford stared back at him with a kind of shock, immobile for a moment.

"He didn't tell me," she said.

I said, "You didn't send him to find her?"

"No," Crawford said, "why would we? She was an adult."

The implication didn't have to be said, but I said it: "Then he had his own reasons."

I let the words sink into them, and then I said, "Felicia might know all that Francesca knew. Some of it, anyway. What motel is she in right now? How far?"

"The Delaware Motel," Martin Crawford said. "Not far."

Katje Crawford stood up. "I'll find Tony, talk to him. I'll find out."

She started from the room before I could move. She walked fast with her athletic stride, and was gone before I realized what she was doing. I began to go after her.

"Let her go," Martin Crawford said.

The pistol in his hand wasn't small. It was a Colt

Agent, a pocket .38 with a two-inch barrel and a lot of power.

"Let her go to Sasser," Crawford said. "She'll find out, or stop him, or whatever has to be done. Only her, Fortune."

He sat down slowly in a big antique chair, the pistol still steady on my chest. I remembered the first time I had met Anthony Sasser in Dresden—when he had been alone in this big house with Katje Crawford while Crawford was at a meeting.

"They're lovers?" I said. "Your wife and Sasser?"

"Yes," Crawford said. "I've known for some time. He's younger, stronger, and he'll go farther than I will. In a way he almost runs the city now, I really work for him. She's been bored with public life for some time. Tony is much more exciting—in business and in private."

"She gets what she wants?" I said.

"Usually," Crawford said, his voice toneless as if he didn't much care. "There are two basic kinds of women, Fortune. One kind wants 'male' attention, needs to have a man want her. She wants his 'maleness,' and she's likely to end up with a hard life. Those women marry the dreamers, the searchers, the wanderers who follow their own destiny all the way. Men who might be gamblers or tycoons; daredevils or hobos; heroes or criminals. It's potluck, win or lose.

"The other kind of woman wants everything a man can give her except his 'maleness.' Status, money, place, appearance, social graces. She judges a man by the position he can give her in the world, his potential to make her life a success. She doesn't care about him as a male, that's peripheral, and she'll do better in life because she chooses the man who will best give her what she wants —the externals. A cool woman concerned with form not substance, and a weak male who will work for form not substance. Katje chose me, and she got what she wanted. I'm a success; important, rich, with position and power. Only sometimes, when such a woman nears forty, she suddenly wants a 'male,' and finds she doesn't have one. She's killed what maleness her man had, and now she has no man. So she finds one. The late passion, the excitement she never wanted."

When he finished his speech, words he must have been saying to himself over and over for years, he seemed to study the blue pistol in his hand as if it was fascinating. He wasn't seeing the pistol. Maybe he was analyzing the quality of his speech; he was a politician, after all. I saw the pistol.

"She'll go to Sasser," I said. "She'll tell him we know he saw Francesca in New York. But we don't know why he went to Francesca, and Felicia is still in Dresden. If Sasser—"

He was up, the pistol down. "The motel, we'll go—"

"No," I said. "I'll go. You go and find Sasser if you can. Find him, and hold him. I'll go to Felicia."

I went out into the rain and to my car.

The Delaware Motel was old and shabby in the rain. The clerk on the desk said that Mr. and Mrs. Paul Two Bears had unit five. Felicia wasn't a halfway girl anymore.

There was light in unit five, and Felicia answered my knock. She had a somber expression, serious, as if she had been talking about serious matters.

"You've found something, Mr. Fortune?" she asked.

"Something," I said.

She still wore her jeans and the sheepskin jacket, they were part of her now. Paul Two Bears sat in a chair. There was no liquor in the room. They had been talking.

I said, "What did you tell your parents, Felicia?"

"Everything," she said, "and nothing. They wanted to know what I was going to do. I don't know what I'm going to do."

"Then why come back here at all?" I said. "Maybe to finish revenging Francesca's murder? Kill the killers?"

Paul Two Bears stood up, but I saw no weapon. Felicia's handbag was on the table. I moved nearer to it.

"Carl Gans was killed with a .22-caliber gun," I said. "At Pine River they'd lie for you, say you'd never left. Do you know that Anthony Sasser found Francesca in New York, and a week later she was dead? Is Sasser next on your list?"

The outside door opened behind me. I didn't turn. The door closed, and Felicia stared over my shoulder. Her face was enough to tell me that the newcomer had a gun on my back.

"Hello, Andera," I said, not turning. "I expected you."

Felicia said, "Who is he? What does he—?"

"My client," I said. "John Andera."

CHAPTER TWENTY-FOUR

John Andera spoke from behind me. "You two leave now."

"Leave?" Felicia Crawford said, and there was alarm in her young face. I saw something else in her face too —a vague, sudden wonder. A tendril of what—recognition? Confused groping on her face. She said, "I'm Felicia Crawford."

"I know who you are," Andera said. "Pack your things. Go on. Don't come back. Both of you."

Paul Two Bears began to pack their few things, throwing the clothes into the two small suitcases. Felicia just stood.

"I want to stay," she said. "I want to talk."

"No," Andera said. "Just get out, now."

I said, "Can I turn around, Andera?"

"Turn around," he said.

He was a few feet inside the closed door. A different man. Instead of his quiet sales-rep's suit, he wore a black jump suit, soft black canvas shoes wet with rain, a black raincoat, and a black soft hat. In the dark he would be invisible. His blue eyes were hard and clear, his face without expression except for a faint, constant twitch at the corner of his left eye—a tension tic, automatic when he was tense, alert. He was looking at Felicia, not at me, and behind his blank expression he was still bleeding inside.

He said, "Go away, Miss Crawford. Don't call the cops if you want Fortune found alive. Go a long way."

"Will he be found alive anyway?" Felicia said, still with that hesitant wisp of recognition, maybe with hope.

"Maybe, and maybe not," Andera said. "I don't know. But if you send the cops, he will be dead. No other way."

I said, "Go on, Felicia. It's too late. Go back to Pine River, or go home, or go anywhere else you can live. Go on."

Paul Two Bears stood with the suitcases. Felicia took his arm, and they walked to the door. As they passed John Andera, she started to speak, but Andera shook his head, jerked his pistol toward the door. He reached out, touched her shoulder with his empty hand. Paul Two Bears took her out.

The door closed, and John Andera sat down. He nodded me to a chair. I sat, and he rested his pistol in his lap. He rubbed at his eyes with both hands as if they hurt. I made no move. The pistol seemed forgotten, but I didn't think it was, and I would have no chance against him. Not him.

"You knew I'd follow," he said. "All that about another man who'd fingered Francesca, about Felicia being in danger, and the act of accusing her here. It was all planned."

"If I'd guessed right, you had to be somewhere near," I said. "You followed me before to Abram Zaremba."

"You're a good detective. That's one reason I hired you. People told me you were good, stubborn."

His voice and manner had changed. Charisma is a word overused in recent years—that personal magic in a man that arouses special loyalty in his followers. Andera had a kind of charisma now. Not leadership, but confidence. He would do his job, all the way. No arrogance or pride, just a fact. If he took a job, it was as good as done. He was a man who lived a double life by reflex. He didn't think about it. In my office he had been John Andera, sales representative. Now he was someone else.

"She's a nice girl," he said, "Felicia. What will she do?"

"She'll be okay. Maybe back to Pine River. Would you like that? It's what you really wanted, wasn't it? Your people, your home. Before Korea, before Katje Van Hoek."

I kept my eyes toward the pistol on his lap, but that was just habit. If he was going to shoot me, I couldn't stop him.

He said, "It's what I've missed most, I guess. The land, the space. It's a rough land, you've seen it. Not fat and soft like here."

"He Who Walked A Black Wind," I said. "A good name. Your father is proud of that name. He's not so proud of Ralph Blackwind as a name, and he wouldn't like John Andera at all."

His smile was thin. "A crazy trick, going out into a tornado like that. I was young. The army made me change the name to Blackwind. Names are magic to us, you know that? When I changed the name, I lost the the magic. The old men would say what happened then had to happen because I lost my name."

"Maybe they're right," I said.

"Why not? It explains as well as anything," he said, and was silent for a moment. "How'd you figure me out? You knew when you came back from Pine River, didn't you? Or maybe you never believed my story from the start."

"No, I believed your story, more or less. It could have been true, and you paid me enough for it to have been all a lie, too. I couldn't decide then."

"When did you decide?"

There was a sense of strangeness, almost eerie, in the way we sat there talking like two casual travelers on some comfortable train rolling through the night toward a distant destination. Both pretending we were oblivious to the pistol in his lap, the murders like a weight on the quiet room.

I said, "I began to notice something—no one had ever seen you with Francesca, no one had ever heard of you. There was no trace of you in her life before the day you walked into my office. You'd made your relation to her as brief and recent as possible, no visits to her place, but someone should have seen you sometime, at least have heard your name. She had a roommate, people were hanging around, watching her. She'd talked, written a few letters. But you didn't show up anywhere, not a whisper. It was strange if your story was true."

"Yeh," he said, as if he'd known the risk.

"Then," I said, "for everyone else there was some outside corroboration of what they told me. Everyone interconnected with past and present and each other—except you. Nothing put you into the picture except your own story. The trail of her father that Francesca followed led to the Emerald Room—but not beyond on any evidence. She was still working there when she died. Only your word said she'd ever talked to you about Raul Negra or Blackwind.

"Your story of meeting her at a party didn't exactly fit. She wasn't after romance or fun, she was hard on her purpose like a hound on a hot scent. There was no hint she'd traced her father beyond the Emerald Room. On the other hand, the story of Raul Negra's big shoot-out made it pretty sure that Blackwind had gone at least one more step after the Emerald Room, but maybe not a step past Abram Zaremba. My hunch was that Blackwind had gone to work for Zaremba in another job back there fifteen years ago—and still had that job. You told me that Zaremba was a part owner of your company.

"I remembered that Katje Crawford had said that Ralph Blackwind had a great love of children. Working for Zaremba, you could hover around Dresden, but keep out of sight. It came to me that Marvel Office Equipment, and you, were that next, last step on the trail. But Francesca hadn't taken the step. She hadn't found you—you had somehow found her. I thought about my being shot outside my office. Why had I been shot at? It looked to me like Sasser, or anyone else, only wanted to know who had hired me. So why shoot me? The answer was that no one had shot at *me,* the shots had been for *you.* Why? Because you were Ralph Blackwind, the real father."

He sat and nodded as if admiring my work, my reasoning. I believed that he was doing just that. He was a professional, a man who appreciated solid work and reasoning.

"Your face is dark enough," I said. "Not too dark, your mother was half Caucasian. Dye takes care of graying, darkens hair. You're taller—probably you wear two-inch lifts in your shoes. The blue eyes are tinted contact lenses. I sensed from the start that your voice had been heavily trained, your speech worked on. Not a recent disguise to fool me, no. You're a fugitive, have been for fifteen years, the disguise is your normal appearance now, part of you, and you had a complete plastic surgery job on your face a long time ago."

"As soon as I had the money and the contacts," he said. "That money Zaremba gave me for saving his bacon the night of the Emerald Room holdup. Zaremba had the contacts, a really good plastic surgeon. I didn't recognize myself after he took care of the scars, the busted bones. He had to make a lot of deep wrinkles, but that just helped. I thought I was home safe, the final piece of luck. Ralph Blackwind was a lucky man after all. It shows that you never know about life."

He sat and rubbed at his eyes again. I guessed that the contact lenses that made his dark eyes blue bothered him when he was tired, disturbed. He said, "Luck. It was all luck after the escape, a fluke. Up at that Catskill lake where we were hiding after the breakout, I ran into a tramp. The fool recognized the prison clothes, tried to capture me. I killed him. I'm an expert, the army taught me well. I changed clothes, dumped him in the lake with my identification on him. I weighted the body, but it didn't sink right away. Chance, you see?

"The two I escaped with ran up just after the body went into the lake. They thought it was me! A fluke. They even tried to swim out, but by then the body sank. That was when I realized that the tramp was my size, weight and build—give or take a few pounds. Just chance again, Fortune. I thought fast, and let my partners go away—thinking I'd drowned. You know the rest. One of them survived, told the cops I'd died in the lake, and in the end the cops believed it."

He touched his pistol, fingered it, as if thinking about the police. "Accident all the way. I guess a man has to have that luck to survive a prison break. That tramp just had no relatives, no friends, was never reported missing. When I'd changed clothes, I'd hoped to gain maybe a day or two, no more. After my partners thought I'd drowned, I figured I might gain even a week. But when I read that the cops had dragged the lake but found no body, I realized they might really believe it was me in that lake. After they didn't find the body for months, I knew I had a real chance. With the plastic surgery, and Zaremba to protect me from being picked up and fingerprinted, I was sure I was safe."

The pain in his eyes was wide as he looked at me. "Safe! Tight, jumpy, careful, never sure. Up in Dresden as often as I could, but really careful. My kids I'd never had a chance to know, to touch. Then Francesca was dead—killed! I had to know who killed her. Damn them to hell!"

I waited until the echo of his violent voice faded in the small room with the rain steady on the trees outside. My eyes were on his pistol, and I was sweating, but I had to say it.

"You had to know," I said, "except that you knew who had killed her from the start."

I could almost see his dark, Indian eyes glitter behind the cloudy blue contact lenses.

I said, "Two of the murders were expert, the work of a professional—because you did them. You're a professional killer, Andera, and you killed Francesca."

CHAPTER TWENTY-FIVE

I said, "If Francesca had found you, you wouldn't have hurt her. You'd have just run again, vanished. You've had a violent life full of killing. You wouldn't shock or stun easily, but that first day in my office you were stunned, in a kind of shock. You were so anxious to hire me to find who had killed Francesca. Why? A fugitive with a prison guard murder hanging over his head had every reason to stay hidden, stay far away from the police, let them handle the murder of even his daughter. But you risked exposing yourself to the police, and to me. You must have had some very powerful reason."

"That she was my daughter isn't enough?" he said.

"No. That would give you sorrow, maybe, but nothing strong enough to risk coming into the open. You had to have a very strong need—like hate," I said. "Remember I said I'd already decided that she hadn't found you, you had found her. But you had *two* newspaper clippings that first day. The first one identified her only as Fran Martin, and if you had known her as Martin, why hadn't you come to me a day earlier? You were stunned, violent to know who had killed her, but you hadn't come to me until after the second news story identified her as Francesca Crawford—your daughter.

"I was sure you hadn't dated her at all, and you hadn't known her as Fran Martin—you would have come a day earlier to me if you had. No, you didn't know Fran Martin at all, not until after she was dead. So why had you clipped the story about the murder of Fran Martin? What was your interest in a girl you'd

never seen or heard of on the day you clipped the story?
Or had you seen her without knowing who she was
until the second story?"

His dark face under the black hat was distracted.
"Yes, what was my connection to a girl named Fran
Martin?"

"None," I said, "unless you were her murderer. A
pro who clipped stories about his victims to keep in-
formed. That second story must have been like being
hit by a train. You were raw and bloody inside when
you came to me. A man who had killed his own daughter. *There* was a reason powerful enough to make you
expose yourself—to find out who had sent you to kill
your own daughter unrecognized in a dark bedroom."

He didn't react, not outwardly, as if all reaction was
gone out of him by now. Maybe it was, or maybe it was
only fifteen years of living as a fugitive always on the
alert. But inside his life was bleeding away.

"You didn't know who had wanted Francesca dead,
did you?" I said. "That was all that explained how you
acted afterward, and that was when it all fit in my mind.
The money you sent to Pine River came at irregular
intervals—when you did a job. A lot of money, so it
was high-paying work. You stayed safe fifteen years in
New York, so you must have had strong protection.
You were so sure of your alibis—because alibis are
part of your trade. The job Abram Zaremba gave you
fifteen years ago was a hired killer!

"A professional killer, that's what you really are, and
you killed Francesca on order. You never know your
victims, do you, that's how it works. This one was
special, I think, but it was routine in one way—you
didn't know exactly who you were sent to kill. I don't
know why you don't know who sent you to kill her, or
why you didn't recognize her—you must have seen her
around Dresden—but that has to be how it happened.
A pretty rotten coincidence. A nightmare."

He had no real reason to be sitting there listening to

me. I wasn't telling him anything important to him. Yet he sat, as if he didn't want to get up, didn't want to do what he had to do to finish what he had started when he hired me.

"No, not a coincidence," he said. "Fate, maybe. Sure, fate. A lot of mistakes, moves, coming together because what I did made them come together. In prison I used to read. Some of those old Greek plays: *Medea, Electra, Antigone.* Fate. Two men meet on a road, one kills the other—it's his brother! All laid down in the cards because they did what they did.

"I had to meet Katje back then when the odds said I'd never get near a woman like her. I had to go off to Korea. She had to toss me over. I had to go after her when I got back. I had to shoot the one person up here who liked me—old Van Hoek. I had to have that crazy luck in the escape. I had to be in the Emerald Room to stop that robbery. Zaremba had to own the Emerald Room, offer me the big job—contract killer. I had to not give a damn back then. What difference did it make, that job, to a hunted guy with a prison-guard murder over him? What did I care about a few more killings if I had protection and good money?"

He gripped his pistol, began to slap it over and over against his leg. "No coincidence, Fortune. I just about set it up, made it have to happen! I took the job Zaremba offered back then partly because it would put me in Dresden a lot, I could be near the kids undercover. I could maybe help them, and see that Katje and Crawford did right by them. With my face fixed I got close to Crawford a few times unknown. Even Katje didn't know me. When I went to meet Tony Sasser a few months ago she was with him. We even shook hands! She didn't know me at all."

"You went to meet Sasser? Why?"

"A job," he said. "See, no coincidence, right? When there was a job in Dresden, Zaremba sent me, naturally.

I was his best killer. I knew Dresden. Who else would he send?"

"You were the man who murdered Mark Leland?"

"Yes," Andera, or Ralph Blackwind, said. "I didn't know his name, or why he had to be hit. I never did. And it didn't have to be Zaremba who wanted a victim dead. The Commissioner sent me on jobs for other guys, you understand?" He seemed to be seeing Abram Zaremba who sent him out to kill for other men. "So I hit Leland. A girl saw me run. Not good enough to hurt me, I was sure, but I holed up in New York anyway. Later, I got word from Zaremba that the girl couldn't finger me, and that was that."

He'd been talking like a man who had to talk, tell. Now, all at once, the words came out stiff. "Three weeks ago Zaremba told me he'd found out that the girl in Dresden had seen more than anyone had thought, maybe did know what I looked like, and was tailing me! Someone had told him that, and Zaremba wanted her shut up for good. He told me where she was living, and I went and killed her!"

His pistol shook, and his knuckles were white where he held it. The control that had kept him going was breaking, raw anguish in his voice now.

"She'd been away in college, I hadn't seen her up here in Dresden for four years. She'd changed. Her looks had changed, she dressed different. I even saw her on the street, planning the hit, making sure it was the roommate who went away and 'Fran Martin' was alone in that apartment. In the room it was dark, and I hit and went. In and out fast. My way. My own daughter!"

I had nothing to say. Condemn him, yes, but he'd done that to himself already. Pity him? Maybe, but how many others had he killed, how many other men's daughters? He was a hired killer, and I felt something as I would for any man who'd lost a child, even Hitler, but that was all. His special anguish was something he would have to face by himself. Excuse—if he could, or if he wanted to. I didn't think he did, no. He had judged himself for his crimes, he expected neither pity nor excuse.

"I had it coming for taking the job fifteen years ago. Okay, sweep me into the garbage. But she didn't have to die! Not my Francesca. Someone else had killed her, too. I was just the knife. I wanted whoever really sent me to kill her!"

His face changed. In that motel room he became the killer, the cunning animal who had survived war, North Korea, prison, and fifteen years on the run. "Remember, I didn't know why I had killed that Mark Leland, or who had wanted him dead. Both times, Leland and Francesca, Commissioner Zaremba could have been sending me out for someone else. He made it sound like that's what he had done. But I couldn't charge around to find out on my own. Someone would know me. So I hired you—and tailed you all the way."

"I spotted you following me once early," I said. "Then you got more careful, and tailed me to Zaremba. I'd told you why Mark Leland had been killed, that Zaremba was personally involved, that he knew who Francesca was, and that probably he'd been the one who wanted her dead. Then you heard the rest when he talked to me up here. When he drugged me, you came in and killed him."

He smiled. "The bastard begged me. Abram Zaremba, a big man with other guy's lives. He said he hadn't known she was my kid, that he'd been told she could identify me, and that she knew he had sent me to kill Leland. He said he was only trying to protect himself —and protect me! I killed him."

I said, "Mark Leland, Francesca, and Abram Zaremba, all your killings. But why kill Carl Gans? Was he the one who told—"

"Not Gans. I didn't touch the bouncer," Andera-

Blackwind said. "He knew me and what I did for work, but he wasn't any part of killing Francesca. Not Carl Gans, no, but I think there's one more who sent me to kill her, right?"

"I don't know," I said. "Listen to me, I—"

"One more," he said, not listening to me. "The one who told Zaremba that Francesca could identify me, was looking for me, could finger Zaremba, too. The one who knew that Francesca was only looking for her father, but who told Zaremba different!"

"Andera," I said, "Or Blackwind, if you go and—"

"John Andera," he said. "Ralph Blackwind died in a prison break fifteen years ago. Or maybe he died earlier when he shot old man Van Hoek. Or maybe in Korea. Or maybe when the white man drafted him and changed his name!"

"Listen to me! We don't know for sure that—"

"Sit up straight, Fortune. Now!"

I sat up straight, he wasn't going to listen. He produced a length of thin rope from inside his black coveralls, the clothes of his dark trade. He began to tie me. He did the job carefully and well, an expert, and he talked while he worked.

"I don't want to kill you too," he said. "One more, and that's the end. I won't be found. Not anywhere. Nothing for Felicia to read in the newspapers about what her father was, what he did with his life."

He tied me solidly, stepped back, pocketed his pistol.

"Thanks for helping, Fortune."

"I'll have to answer for that," I said. "How long can you run?"

"As long as I have to, and as far. I've been running all my life, but not much longer. In the garbage with me, right? Good riddance."

I didn't bother to reason with him anymore, and he gagged me, and went out the door. He backed out, watching me, and faded into the night and rain like a vanishing ghost.

CHAPTER TWENTY-SIX

Only minutes had passed when I heard the sound. Someone was outside the motel room in the rain.

The door opened. Felicia Crawford stood there. She came in, slim and young, and removed my gag.

"Untie me. Maybe there's time."

She began to untie my ropes. "He's my father, isn't he?"

"Where's Two Bears?" I said.

"In our car outside. I knew that man was my father. I made Paul stay close and wait. I knew he wouldn't hurt you."

"I didn't," I said, rubbed at my wrists as she got the ropes off. "Go somewhere, Felicia. Anywhere."

"You said there might be time? Time for what?"

She had the ropes off my legs. I stood up. "Time to stop him from killing anyone else. He's a killer, Felicia. Many times over—cold and for pay. He had bad breaks, cruel breaks, but he failed himself, too. Old Two Bears Walk Near is right. Your father had a choice, if a hard one, but some weakness in him matched what the world did to him, and his anger turned bad. He's doomed, Felicia. Forget him. Tell me where Anthony Sasser lives."

She told me. It wasn't too far from the Crawford house.

"He's my father," she said. "I want to talk to him, for Francesca. It was important to her."

I couldn't tell her the truth, no, she'd find out soon enough. "What was important to Francesca was a man eighteen years ago. A man and his life. You can still have that life, and he'd want you to—his life back at Pine River. Go there if you want your father. That's where he really is."

Paul Two Bears spoke from the doorway. "He's right. That man wasn't my uncle. Even his eyes are a lie."

She stood there torn between what we said, and the need to know her real father at least for an instant. I had no time to wait. I didn't know what Andera had heard, or thought he had heard. I couldn't be sure who his last victim was to be.

I ran for my car.

Anthony Sasser's house was smaller than the Crawford's, farther back from the road, and dark. There was no light in it anywhere, and the green Cadillac was not there. Neither was any other car Katje Crawford might have come in, or John Andera.

I drove on to the Crawford mansion. Martin Crawford was in the living room when the maid let me in. His face looked like he had lost fifty pounds in the last hours. Old Mrs. Van Hoek sat in a chair as if she were trying to stay unseen. I pulled out my big pistol. I aimed it at Crawford.

"Hand me your gun," I said to Crawford. "By the barrel."

He didn't protest. I pocketed the Colt Agent.

"Is he here?" I said. "Sasser?"

"No. He wasn't at his house or his office. I tried his club, too. Nowhere. Katje isn't back, either. Is Felicia—?"

"She's okay," I said, and told him the whole thing fast.

He sat down. "My God. Ralph . . . John Andera, you say? He killed Francesca? His own . . . My God."

"He's been around here in the background for years. He says he saw you, and you saw him. You never knew?"

"I never saw anyone like Ralph Blackwind, no! I thought he was dead, I never considered if anyone could be Ralph. He was watching, and then . . . ?"

I turned to the old woman, Mrs. Van Hoek. "Your husband knew Blackwind was alive. Did you know?"

The old woman shrank away from me in her chair. She watched Martin Crawford.

"Tell him what he wants to know, Mother," Crawford said.

Her eyes were blank. "I didn't know. Emil always liked Ralph Blackwind, even after Ralph shot him."

"Your husband told Francesca something. That Blackwind was alive, yes, but what else?"

"I don't know," Mrs. Van Hoek said.

"He almost died, he knew Blackwind was alive, yet he never told. He protected an escaped murderer who'd shot him, tried to kidnap Katje and the girls, nearly killed them? Why?" I said. "Tell me just what did happen that night eighteen years ago."

The old woman shook her head, no. She was afraid.

"Tell him," Martin Crawford said from his chair.

When she spoke then, it was like a robot. "We were in the old house. Ralph came. He had guns. He was violent, in a rage. Katje tried to run away. Ralph shot everywhere, with both his guns. A pistol and a submachine gun. One in each hand. He smashed the living room mirror, the lamps, the windows. Emil pushed me down behind a couch. He lay there with me. Katje said she would go with Ralph. She got the children. Ralph made us stay down on the floor out of sight. We didn't move, Emil and I. They all went out. We heard them drive away. Emil got up from behind the couch. We heard their car stop at the end of the street. Ralph ran back. Emil started to the door. Ralph shot him through the broken window. Emil was badly hurt. A few moments later their car drove away and was gone. Martin came home ten minutes later. He stopped Emil's bleeding, got a doctor, called the police. They caught Ralph in Utica. Katje had managed to call the police while Ralph was asleep."

She finished it there. I imagined the violent scene that night—Blackwind half-crazy, firing a submachine gun with one hand, a pistol with the other. Smashing the house in his rage.

"Katje called?" I said. "She turned him in to the police."

"What else could she do? He was violent, dangerous," Crawford said from his chair.

I watched him. "Is that how it happened, Crawford? Did she tell it exactly?"

"I don't know," he said. "I arrived ten minutes later."

"Did you?" I said. "Or maybe ten minutes earlier?"

He said, "No. They were gone when I got there. Only the Van Hoeks were there, Emil bleeding on the floor."

"Almost dead," I said. "Yet he learned later that Blackwind was still alive, had made his escape from prison, and he never told anyone. Why? Why protect a man who'd almost killed him?"

Crawford shook his head. "I don't know, Fortune."

"You're sure you weren't there earlier, Crawford? What did ballistics say about the bullets that shot Emil Van Hoek?"

"From Ralph Blackwind's pistol. It was an 8-mm Nambu he'd picked up in North Korea. No mistake possible, a rare gun here. There wasn't another one in Dresden, I don't think."

"His pistol?" I said. "Not the submachine gun?"

"No."

I said, "You told the story just that way at the trial? Emil Van Hoek, and Mrs. Van Hoek there, told the story?"

"They weren't at the trial. There was no need. Emil was too sick. Katje testified, and Blackwind admitted going crazy, shooting up the house. The Van Hoeks gave depositions."

"Depositions?" I said. "Where would Sasser and Katje be, Crawford? Think? Where could Sasser be now?"

"I don't know," he said, squeezed his hands together in that chair. "I've thought, but I can't—"

Old Mrs. Van Hoek said, "She meets with Sasser at the lodge on Black Mountain Lake. Abram Zaremba's lodge. She goes there to him sometimes."

Crawford began to say something, but I didn't wait. I ran out to my car. The rain had stopped now. I drove toward Black Mountain Lake and the million-dollar project that, in one way, had started the whole tragedy. The project, and Joel Pender's drunken stupidity. In one way they had started it all, but in reality it had begun a long time ago when a young Indian soldier married a patroon girl momentarily rejecting her heritage and future for passion. A moment that she had regretted, and started the whole inexorable chain of violence.

Black Mountain Lake glittered darkly like the surface of Pluto with its methane ocean. There was light in the lodge at the end of the county-built private road. I saw the three cars. One was Anthony Sasser's green Cadillac. I drew my gun, and slipped up to a window of the lodge. I knew who the third car had to belong to. Maybe I wasn't too late. But I was.

Through the window I saw a large, rustic room. Katje Crawford stood against a far wall in her red slack suit, her handbag held in both hands before her like a shield. John Andera faced her some ten feet away with his gun in his hand. They didn't seem to be speaking, just looking at each other with closed faces, the death of their daughter, and eighteen years, between them.

Something more lay between them, too. Something real, physical. The body of Anthony Sasser.

Sasser lay on his back in a pool of blood, his dead

eyes fixed on the ceiling with surprise and fear. He was dead, John Andera knew how to kill, did not miss.

I slipped around to the front door. It was open. I went inside silently. John Andera heard me when I was twenty feet away in the rustic room, and half behind him to his left.

"I've got my gun, Andera," I said.

I hoped my voice wasn't shaking. I couldn't play with him. If he moved, I'd have to shoot. If I gave him one chance, I was as good as dead.

His eyes looked toward me.

CHAPTER TWENTY-SEVEN

John Andera looked toward me, and then back at Katje Crawford, and let his gun drop away from him with a small toss. Too dead inside now to even try to run and end it all his own way if that meant more struggle. My stomach relaxed. I went limp. I hadn't been so sure I was any match for him even with my gun and the advantage.

"Shoot him," Katje Crawford said. "He's a murderer ten times over. Shoot him now."

"I'll take him in," I said.

"He'll fool you," she said. "He shot Tony in cold blood."

Andera said, "Sasser admitted it, Fortune. He was scared, he talked. He told Zaremba that Francesca had really seen my face when I killed Leland, that she was working with the police, that she knew Leland had been killed to protect the Black Mountain Lake project. He made Zaremba send me to kill Fran."

His dead eyes turned toward Katje Crawford. She still stood against the wall in that red slack suit, fear and a kind of hate on her face.

"I didn't know it was Francesca," Andera said to her. "I didn't recognize her. I killed those who made me do it."

Katje Crawford opened her handbag and took out a cigarette. Her hands shook, she could barely light the cigarette. Her eyes seemed hypnotized by John Andera's face, watching only him.

I said, "Did Sasser tell you why he did it, Andera?"

178

Katje Crawford looked at me now. The look was one of sheer terror.

"What?" John Andera said.

"Did Sasser tell you why he told Zaremba that Francesca was dangerous? It was all a lie. Francesca didn't see your face when you killed Leland, she couldn't identify you. She wasn't holding anything back, she had no evidence against you or Zaremba. All she was doing was looking for her real father. Nothing else. So what reason did Sasser have to lie to Zaremba and get her killed?"

It was so silent in that big lodge room that I could hear the cars on the distant county highway, and the slow drip of the last drops of the stopped rain from the trees outside.

Andera said, "He had his reasons, Fortune. He did it. He told me he did it."

"He did it," I said. "The question is why?"

Katje Crawford said, "He was sure Francesca knew too much. He told me that."

She smoked, the cigarette trembling in her frightened hand like a rabbit shivering in the open as a fox stalked. I spoke to John Andera.

"I told Katje there that Sasser had talked to Francesca in New York. You heard me tell her tonight, didn't you, Andera? You were outside the Crawford house listening. I told her, and she came running to Sasser. Why? They were lovers, Andera. She was tossing over Crawford, as she tossed you over twenty years ago. But she didn't come here just to warn Sasser."

Katje Crawford said, "Stop it, Fortune."

I said, "All Francesca was doing was looking for her real father. That's all. The rest was lies, a smoke screen set up by Sasser—and by Katje."

I turned to face Katje Crawford. "You told Sasser to lie to Zaremba and have Francesca killed."

She shook her head sharply. "You're wrong. She was my daughter. You're terribly wrong."

"A daughter you were never close to, always hated. Both the twins, really, because they were as much a part of Blackwind as they were of you. But Francesca mostly because she was most like her real father, because she sensed your hate of her, your fear. Since she was a little girl she was different, against you, sensed the wall between you. A wall of hate and fear because you've always been afraid Blackwind would someday come back. You never believed he died in that escape. Death, Katje, that's what you're afraid of. The fear of being killed if Blackwind ever found out the real truth."

Katje Crawford smoked, drew the smoke deep into her lungs. John Andera watched her. I moved closer to him.

"After Francesca left home," I said, "Katje found out what old Emil Van Hoek had told Francesca. We'll never know if she killed old Van Hoek, too, or if he just died under the strain. A little of both, maybe. But, whatever, Katje was terrified of what would happen if Francesca got to you and told you what she had learned from Emil Van Hoek.

"You see, she *had* recognized you that time you went to Sasser about the contract to kill Leland. I don't know how, but she did. Then Francesca went looking for you, and Katje had to stop her. She got Sasser to locate Francesca, and he did. Then she had him tell Zaremba that Francesca was dangerous, that Zaremba had to stop her. What Katje and Sasser hadn't expected was that Zaremba would send you to kill your own daughter! Chance, accident, call it fate again.

"Then I showed up hired by someone. They had to know who hired me. Sasser tailed me to find out, and spotted you that morning in front of my office. He knew who you were, and what you were, and what had happened. He knew you were trying to find out who had made you kill Francesca, so he tried to shoot you, but got me instead. Then you killed Zaremba, and they really panicked. They had set Francesca up for murder, you had killed her, and now you were after them. They didn't dare risk *me* finding it all out, so Katje killed Carl Gans who could have led me to the truth. Only he lived just too long. He told me enough."

Andera said, "What could Francesca have told me?"

I looked at Katje Crawford. It was, after all, her story. She said nothing, stubbed out her cigarette in an ashtray as if unaware of what she was doing. A reflex action, neat and orderly, a well-mannered woman. Andera was close to me now, his false blue eyes staring into my face, waiting.

I shrugged. "That you didn't shoot Emil Van Hoek back there eighteen years ago. The one crime you couldn't evade. The charge that sent you to prison and ruined your life, and you never did it. You shot up that room at random. Emil Van Hoek fell behind the couch. You didn't see him again, did you? You left with Katje and the children. You drove off. But you stopped at the end of the street, and—"

Andera said, "Katje ran back. She said she had dropped some medicine the kids had to have. She ran back, I waited in the car. I had the kids, they were crying, the motor was running, I—"

"You were distracted, not thinking about gunshots. The kids were noisy, a Nambu makes little noise. Katje had your pistol with her, easy to grab it in the confusion, you had put down the guns to drive. Later, at the trial, you assumed you'd hit old Van Hoek in that first volley of wild shots in the room. Van Hoek never came to court. But he knew who had shot him."

I faced Katje Crawford. "What was your father to do back then? His own daughter had shot him, but could he send her to prison, ruin her life and her children's lives? So he never told. He kept silent, and felt guilty all these years. That was why he didn't reveal that he knew Ralph Blackwind was alive, and that was why he finally told the truth to Francesca.

He was near death, she was aware of her real father at last from Joel Pender's mistake, so he told her, and that was why you had her killed."

Katje Crawford's eyes had the fear in them, and the hate, too, and a kind of strangely detached anger—at a world that wouldn't behave as she insisted it should. How dare the world not do what she wanted? Then and now. It was the world's fault, Ralph Blackwind's fault for not understanding back then that she had had to correct a mistake, the fault of Francesca for being the intransigent child she had been.

"You had to come back," she said to Andera. "Ruin my life. So insane you thought I'd actually go with you that night, never even noticed that I took your pistol back to the house. Yes, I shot my father. I hoped I'd killed him! You would have gone to the electric chair then! He didn't die, but he didn't tell, either. It was fine. Only the old fool had to tell Francesca three months ago! He wanted her to know the truth about her real father before he died. He told her. And I knew you were really alive. I'd seen you." '

She glared at Andera; it was his fault for being alive.

"I didn't recognize you at all," she said. "But you have a habit. A strange, unique habit—you always smell a drink before you drink it. When I saw you do that with Tony Sasser that night at his house, I knew. I couldn't believe it, but I knew it was you."

Andera said, "At Pine River we smell the water we drink. Alkali; poisoned water holes. I never lost the habit."

"Once I saw that," Katje Crawford said, "I saw the contact lenses, the dyed hair, the lifts in your shoes, the hint of the face I knew under the changes. You were alive, and then my father told Francesca the truth. To clear his conscience! Was I going to let her tell you, let you come for me? A professional killer?"

John Andera moved. I had relaxed too much. He lunged, and he had my gun. Without a word, he lunged, got hold of my gun, and for an instant we wrestled. The gun fell from my hand, hit the floor with a loud clatter. Silent, he jumped toward where it had fallen.

We both saw the little automatic come out of Katje Crawford's handbag. She held it, the .22-caliber mate of the one Felicia had aimed at me. The pistol that had killed Carl Gans. Both Andera and I stood motionless for a moment. Then Andera forgot my pistol, began to walk straight toward her, his hands curled as if for her throat.

She shot him four times. All four shots hit him in the chest and stomach. He walked on. She shot a fifth time. He stumbled to one knee, sank forward on his face not three feet from her with his hands still reaching toward her.

That fifth shot was all that saved my life. She shot me in the stomach. I doubled over, but the little bullet didn't stop me. I was on my knees reaching toward my gun on the floor. She tried to shoot again, but the gun was empty. Andera's pistol was ten feet from her. She couldn't get it before I reached my gun. She turned and ran out of the lodge. I got my pistol, and fired one shot before she vanished. It went somewhere in the ceiling.

Outside, her car started, faded away.

I crawled to John Andera. He had rolled onto his back. He was still breathing. His eyes were open up toward the ceiling, but not seeing the ceiling. Seeing, maybe, the sky of Arizona.

"Andera?" I said. "Blackwind?"

"Trapped . . ." his whisper said ". . . the land . . ."

That was all he said. I crawled to the telephone, called the police. When I crawled back to him, He Who Walked A Black Wind was dead.

CHAPTER TWENTY-EIGHT

I was in the hospital for two weeks. The little bullet had torn me up inside, and they weren't sure I would make it. I just lay there and breathed. I cared about nothing except staying alive—just like Katje Crawford.

Lieutenant Oster wasn't happy with me, neither was Gazzo down in New York. But the police must work on facts and evidence, and this time there had been no other way to smoke out the truth except my way. They could close the books now in both cities—there was no point to charging Harmon Dunstan or George Tabor, the dead Mark Leland's partner, for their silence and evasion.

My girl, Marty, came up to see me. She had her director with her, so we could only be polite. Mayor Martin Crawford visited me on the sixth day. I was feeling better, I knew I would live a while. Crawford told me that they hadn't found Katje yet. He seemed older, sadder.

"They traced her to Los Angeles," he said. "Poor Katje, she must have been crazy with fear. I don't know what I'm going to tell the children, the younger ones."

"Try the truth," I said. "What happens to Black Mountain Lake now? Any second thoughts?"

"Of course not. Someone will take over for Abram Zaremba."

"Business as usual, as soon as you know who to cozy up to?"

"What happened had no relation to the project, Fortune," he said. "I had no part in what happened."

184

"You could have told Francesca the truth all these years, you could have been a father. But you kept quiet, got your share."

"It was all Katje's ideas and actions."

"But you wanted her, so you share the guilt. At least you could be a real mayor, work for the people, not for the Sassers and Zarembas. That had its part in killing Francesca, too. The legal but immoral world you live with. Greed and privilege."

"I do nothing wrong, Fortune. A man exists in his world. I work with things as they are, get all I can. I live today, win if I can, and don't apologize for the way things are."

He wouldn't change, no. Self-interest was the base. He'd get a new wife someday, one just like Katje, but without, hopefully, a mistake in her past that drove her to hate, fraud, fear and murder. He'd forget Francesca because it was too hard, too unnerving, to go on remembering. Eventually, he would come to think of her as a sad, foolish girl with wild ideas that got her killed— her fault, not the world's.

Near the end of my two weeks in hospital, Lieutenant Oster brought the word that Katje Crawford had been found in Panama City. She had tried to shoot the Panamanian policemen, still fighting for her life and her needs. They shot her to pieces. They don't fool with armed fugitives down there.

It all seemed so purposeless—Katje Crawford's battles for her privileges; Zaremba and Sasser's scheming for power and money; Martin Crawford's deals for his big house and his comfort. No purpose beyond the moment. All so brief and transient in a life that was itself so transient you had to give it shape with some purpose or there was only a mad race going nowhere.

On my last day, as I dressed, Felicia Crawford and Paul Two Bears came to visit. The police had told them all of it. Felicia's face was dry and quiet. Almost as quiet as the face of Francesca on the morgue slab where it had all started for me. It gave my healing stomach a turn, seeing Felicia's face so much like that of her dead sister.

"So?" I said. "Can you forget it all?"

"I don't know," she said. "We're going back to Pine River. I like it there—the space, the land; hard as it is. I'm half Indian, after all. Work with the tribe, the land."

"A purpose?" I said.

Paul Two Bears said, "For the old man, before he dies."

"A change is coming," Felicia said. "For the Indians, maybe for the country. Maybe they'll listen to the Indians, to us. The old man thinks the time is near."

"I envy you," I said.

"A home," she said. "A real home. Not a father, maybe, but a grandfather, an uncle, cousins, a place. For me and for Francesca. I'll be happy for both of us. I know who we are, what we are. For both of us, Mr. Fortune."

"She'd be glad," I said.

She would be—Francesca Blackwind. Aware, somehow, all her short life that she belonged somewhere.

After they had gone, before I went out and back to my own narrow world, I sat and pictured again Francesca's dead face in the morgue. She would be happy to know that her sister had gone home, had found the place that she, Francesca, had known was there and had wanted.

Out of it all, one had gone home, had found the lost home they had carried inside them. It made me feel almost good.

ABOUT THE AUTHOR

Michael Collins is the pseudonym of Dennis Lynds, a novelist and short-story writer. "Collins," he says, "is more than a pen name; he is my alter ego—part of me that isn't the same man who writes my other books. I live far from New York now, but Collins will never leave that complex city-world where everything changes and yet never changes. When I decided to write about Dan Fortune, his city and his people, I knew I needed Michael Collins—the perpetual New Yorker no matter where he is."

With time out for war service, colleges, residence in Europe and wandering across the country, Mr. Lynds has lived most of his life in Dan Fortune's city.

FINE MYSTERY AND SUSPENSE
TITLES FROM CARROLL & GRAF

☐ Bentley, E.C./TRENT'S OWN CASE	$3.95
☐ Blake, Nicholas/MURDER WITH MALICE	$3.95
☐ Blake, Nicholas/A TANGLED WEB	$3.50
☐ Boucher, Anthony/THE CASE OF THE BAKER STREET IRREGULARS	$3.95
☐ Boucher, Anthony (ed.)/FOUR AND TWENTY BLOODHOUNDS	$3.95
☐ Brand, Christianna/FOG OF DOUBT	$3.50
☐ Brand, Christianna/TOUR DE FORCE	$3.95
☐ Brown, Fredric/THE LENIENT BEAST	$3.50
☐ Brown, Fredric/THE SCREAMING MIMI	$3.50
☐ Browne, Howard/THIN AIR	$3.50
☐ Burnett, W.R./LITTLE CAESAR	$3.50
☐ Butler, Gerald/KISS THE BLOOD OFF MY HANDS	$3.95
☐ Carr, John Dickson/THE BRIDE OF NEWGATE	$3.95
☐ Carr, John Dickson/CAPTAIN CUT-THROAT	$3.95
☐ Carr, John Dickson/DARK OF THE MOON	$3.50
☐ Carr, John Dickson/THE DEVIL IN VELVET	$3.95
☐ Carr, John Dickson/THE EMPEROR'S SNUFF-BOX	$3.50
☐ Carr, John Dickson/FIRE BURN	$3.50
☐ Carr, John Dickson/IN SPITE OF THUNDER	$3.50
☐ Carr, John Dickson/LOST GALLOWS	$3.50
☐ Carr, John Dickson/NINE WRONG ANSWERS	$3.50
☐ Chesterton, G.K./THE CLUB OF QUEER TRADES	$3.95
☐ Chesterton, G.K./THE MAN WHO KNEW TOO MUCH	$3.95
☐ Chesterton, G.K./THE MAN WHO WAS THURSDAY	$3.50
☐ Coles, Mannning/ALL THAT GLITTERS	$3.95
☐ Coles, Manning/THE FIFTH MAN	$2.95

☐	MacDonald, Philip/THE RASP	$3.50
☐	Mason, A.E.W./AT THE VILLA ROSE	$3.50
☐	Mason, A.E.W./THE HOUSE IN LORDSHIP LANE	$3.50
☐	Maston, A.E.W./THE HOUSE OF THE ARROW	$3.50
☐	Priestley, J.B./SALT IS LEAVING	$3.50
☐	Queen, Ellery/THE FINISHING STROKE	$3.95
☐	Rogers, Joel T./THE RED RIGHT HAND	$3.50
☐	'Sapper'/BULLDOG DRUMMOND	$3.50
☐	Siodmak, Curt/DONOVAN'S BRAIN	$3.50
☐	Symons, Julian/THE 31st OF FEBRUARY	$3.50
☐	Symons, Julian/BLAND BEGINNING	$3.95
☐	Symons, Julian/BOGUE'S FORTUNE	$3.95
☐	Symons, Julian/THE BROKEN PENNY	$3.95
☐	Wainwright, John/ALL ON A SUMMER'S DAY	$3.50
☐	Wallace, Edgar/THE FOUR JUST MEN	$2.95
☐	Woolrich, Cornell/VAMPIRE'S HONEYMOON	$3.50

Available from fine bookstores everywhere or use this coupon for ordering:

Caroll & Graf Publishers, Inc., 260 Fifth Avenue, N.Y., N.Y. 10001

Please send me the books I have checked above. I am enclosing $_____ (please add $1.75 per title to cover postage and handling.) Send check or money order—no cash or C.O.D.'s please. N.Y. residents please add 8¼% sales tax.

Mr/Mrs/Miss _____

Address _____

City _____ State/Zip _____

Please allow four to six weeks for delivery.
